Unrelenting Nightmare

Jennifer dreamed...

... of men and women who gathered at the foot of her bed and, with shrill laughter, tore off their faces to reveal beneath the feces of creatures that looked like wolves, tore off their clothes to reveal the wolf fur beneath, then reached out their clawed hands to pull at her cheeks, her brow, her hair, then drag her to a mirror where she saw, in her reflection . . .

the face of a wolf snarling back at her . . .

iBooks in the **PRIVATE SCHOOL**™ Series

Most iBooks are available at special quantity discounts for bulk purchases for sales promotions, premiums or fundraising. Special books or book excerpts can also be created to fit specific needs.

For details, email the publisher
@bricktower@aol.com

PRIVATE SCHOOL
#5

THE ENEMY WITHIN

Steven Charles

A BYRON PREISS VISUAL PUBLICATIONS, INC.
BOOK

iBooks
Habent Sua Fata Libelli

iBooks
Manhanset House
Dering Harbor, New York 11965

bricktower@aol.com • www.ibooksinc.com

Library of Congress Cataloging-in-Publication Data
Charles, Steven. The enemy within.
        (Private School) "A Byron Preiss book."
p. cm.
        [1. Young Adult Fiction—Horror. 2. Young Adult Fiction—Science Fiction—Alien Contact. 3. Young Adult Fiction—Werewolfs and Shifters.] I. Lang, Gary, iII. II. Title. III.
        Series: Charles, Steven. Private School.

ISBN 978-1-59687-734-4
December 2018

SPECIAL THANKS TO RON BUEHL,
PAT MACDONALD, MARJORIE HANLON,
AND DAVID M. HARRIS.
EDITOR—RUTH ASHBY

THE ENEMY WITHIN

Table of Contents

One

SOMETHING WAS DOWN THERE.

Jennifer crouched behind a bush and peered through its nearly bare branches to the trail she and her friends had followed to the top of the steep, wooded hill. Below, to the narrow wedge of ground that separated that hill from the next, there were nothing but rocks. Scattered boulders. Low brush that clung stubbornly to places where the earth was barely deep enough to support the roots. A switchback climb that had taken the four of them nearly an hour to complete in the darkness.

It was quiet now.

Too quiet.

Something was down there.

She was sure of it.

Her vision blurred slightly, and she wiped her eyes gently with the sleeve of her coat. She shifted her feet to ease the strain of her position, and she winced when a pebble was dislodged and skittered down the slope, sounding to her like a hundred men running over broken glass.

She held her breath.

And released it with a silent sigh when the quiet returned and she could hear nothing but the soft soughing of the breeze through the clearing behind her. A

1

swallow. She looked up into the slight autumn haze that dulled the colors of the leaves, faded the blue of the sky, and added to the chill the breeze carried on its back. A look down to a worn trail, a reminder of the deer and other animals that had passed through there for centuries.

She had heard the sounds only a few minutes before and at first thought her fears had been feeding her imagination. But when she had heard the sounds again, furtive and cautious, she rose from her bed of leaves and moved swiftly to the bush, looked down and waited.

It was difficult to see much. The morning sun hadn't yet risen high enough to drive all the shadows from that side of the hill. They still filled the gaps between the boulders, still slid down the narrow almost nonexistent path she and the others had followed.

Anything could be down there.

Including the alien creatures that had driven them into the forest.

A chill raced along her spine, and she drew the collar of her jacket close over her throat.

Another stone skittered down the slope.

The last time she had seen one of the wolf-beasts, it had been fighting with Conrad and Lee in a clearing near its den. It had won, but inexplicably vanished without killing them all. As it could have done. As it had done to others.

A crow wheeled and cawed overhead.

And the only help she and her friends had, had been Jack Rumbel, an overweight detective who had fled in the middle of the struggle.

The wolf-creature, the alien, had left them with a warning, one that had eventually sent them running deep into the woods.

You have no place to go now.

And at the time they had believed it.

A twig snapped, and she tensed. There was no mistake now—she did see movement down there, just past a large boulder midway along the slope.

She blinked, rubbed her eyes, and tried to practice what Conrad had taught her—never stare at a place straight on when you're waiting for something to show itself. Look to one side so your vision won't trick you. If something really does move, you'll know it.

She glanced over her shoulder, trying to catch Lee's eye. But he was kneeling in front of Conrad and Marysue, his back to her, the others' concentration on whatever he was drawing on the ground with a stick.

When she looked back, the shadow of a small cloud rippled down the slope, gliding, blending, finally vanishing into the trees below. And as she followed the shadow, she saw the movement again, not a shadow but something large enough to be one of *them.*

She held her breath.

Her left hand plucked up a stone and tossed it over her shoulder.

There was shifting down there behind the boulder.

A rock tumbled into the brush.

She threw another stone behind her without looking, not daring to take her gaze from the spot below. A grunt and a muffled curse were all the answer she was to receive. She signaled wildly with her hand. Immediately there was silence behind her, broken only by someone trying to cross to her without making a sound.

A hand on her shoulder.

A quick look—it was Lee Fawkes.

She pointed to the boulder and mouthed, "Something is down there."

It was morning, but suddenly it felt like midnight.

Lee lightly put a hand on her arm, and she could sense Conrad Chang and Marysue Beauford making their way toward them. She glanced over her shoulder and saw them carrying branches, weapons they had picked up in the forest during their flight. Marysue looked frightened; Conrad grim. They stopped a few yards to her left and crouched behind an evergreen shrub.

Another shifting.

Another fall of stones from below, so loud in the silence that it sounded like a landslide.

Oh, no, she thought. There's more than one.

Lee's grip tightened.

Now there was a skittering as though whatever was coming after them had lost its balance. A scrabbling. A branch cracking in two.

Then it came around the boulder, and Jennifer leaped to her feet, not realizing until she did that she had a large rock in her right hand.

"Oh, no!" she said out loud.

And the young stag looked up at her, the doe beside it wide-eyed and fearful.

For almost a full minute they stared at one another without moving. Finally the stag snorted and flipped up its tail in a signal of danger, and the two deer plunged back down the slope, leaping over rocks, veering from side to side until they vanished into the trees.

The crow cawed and soared over the far hill.

No one said a word until Jennifer dropped her rock, shook her head, and shambled back into the clearing. She found it hard to catch her breath, and she gulped at the air, her face lifted toward the sky. Her legs were weak, her arms were like lead, and she knew that it was impossible to go on like that any longer.

Even if it meant walking straight into the hands of the monsters who waited for them.

Conrad returned to sit cross-legged on a half-buried boulder, elbows on his knees and palms cupping his cheeks. Marysue sat heavily beside him, a hand on his shoulder, which she absently massaged while taking deep, shuddering breaths and staring blindly at the sky. Lee was to their left, huddled in his denim jacket, miserably shaking his head.

They'd had nothing to eat in the two days and three nights they'd been in the woods, except for a few candy bars that Conrad always had with him; nothing to drink except for water from a brook that trickled not far from a cabin near Witch's Eye where they had first gone for shelter. And at night the temperature had dropped so low they had had to burrow under the leaves for warmth.

The morning chill would ease as the sun continued to climb, but it wouldn't be enough to drive the cold from their bones. They had lit no fire the night before, nor on the other nights they had spent in the woods.

Jennifer supposed it didn't matter how uncomfortable they were as long as they were still alive.

But if they remained out there much longer, she wasn't sure that "alive" would accurately describe them.

Leaves rustled.

A twig snapped.

Something small scurried through the underbrush.

She thought about the deer and uttered a barking laugh she smothered as soon as the others looked at her and frowned.

"We were ready to brain a stupid deer," she said, the sound of her voice too loud. "I guess that makes our decision for us, don't you think?"

"Yeah," said Lee. "I guess it does."

"Well," Marysue said, clapping her hands once and pushing herself to her feet. "It's about time. This girl is about to waste away to nothing. She was not meant to live like Daniel Boone, you know. She was meant to be pampered, waited on, and generally spoiled."

The sense of relief that flooded the clearing was as brisk as the breeze that gusted through just then. Lee smiled; Conrad, as he stood, stretched and grinned; and Marysue made a show of combing her fingers through her matted dark hair.

Then Lee walked over to Jennifer and took her hands. "You all right?"

She couldn't quite smile. "I think so."

"It's the only thing we can do, Jen. We can't hide out here now. We have to leave, organize, and get ready to fight. You know that."

"I know."

You have no place to go now.

They thought that Thaler Academy, the private school Jennifer and Marysue attended, would have been closed to them because the police, thanks to Rumbel, would be convinced they were a gang of thieves, working the town of Staines. Conrad's and Lee's homes had been out, they decided, because the police and the aliens would have been watching them, waiting for them to show up.

So they had had no choice but to run blindly into the woods until they could run no farther.

But the night before Jennifer had given voice to what they knew was their only choice.

"But what," she asked, strangely fearful now, "if they are waiting for us?"

"They're always going to be waiting for us," Conrad reminded her. "Until we do something about it, they're always going to be there. And we agreed that we can't do anything about it out here. We have to leave here and organize."

"Yes, but—"

"But nothing," Marysue said. "Remember, Field, this was your brilliant idea."

Jennifer couldn't help it—she grinned. And softened the grin to a smile when Lee spilled his arms around her and gave her a quick hug.

"So let's get going," he said. "I would kill for a decent bed right now."

"Watch your mouth, Fawkes," Marysue said.

Lee released Jennifer and went over to Conrad to talk with him about which was the best way to get to their destination.

Marysue looked at the ground as if thinking about cleaning up before leaving; she grinned when she saw Jennifer watching.

"Habit," the Virginian drawled. "My mother always told me to make my bed before I went out."

Jennifer grinned back and kicked hard at the leaves she had used to cover herself the night before. When Beauford did the same, they both broke into laughter and raced around the clearing, kicking, giggling, finally dropping to the ground in nervous exhaustion. They pulled up their knees to cradle themselves. Rocking.

"You know," Jennifer said, "I thought Rumbel would have had the cops out here looking for us."

"I didn't," Marysue said. "That man was scared to death. I'm willing to bet he's convinced himself it was a dream. Or that we had someone in costume, like he thought at first."

And then Marysue asked what they'd all been thinking since the night they had taken flight: "But why haven't the aliens chased us?"

The only answer Jennifer could think of didn't quite settle the question: "They aren't afraid of us. They think they can take care of us if we try to come at them again."

The boys walked over to them then.

"Okay," Conrad said. "We think we can do it."

"Think has nothing to do with it," Marysue told him as she jumped to her feet. "If we don't do it right, we're in our graves, Zucco. And I hate funerals," she snapped.

"Maybe," Lee said, "we ought to stop talking and get moving."

Jennifer agreed, and they took the southern slope of the hill. None of them looked back. Only the boys had experience in the wooded hills around Staines—the nearest town to the academy—and that was limited. But they were counting on two things to get them to their destination safely: that neither the police nor the aliens had extensive search parties out looking for them, and neither would expect them to go where they were heading.

If they were wrong, the consequences were unthinkable.

If they were right, then Jennifer knew they had at least a small chance to prevent the aliens from spreading their influence any further.

And that small hope was all they needed to spur them on.

So Jennifer said nothing to Lee or the others when she heard something pacing them in the trees.

A deer, she told herself. It's only a deer.

Progress through the thick woods was so slow that the boys finally decided to use one of the hiking trails that had been worn bare by generations of Staines Boy and Girl Scouts. They hit the trail almost at a run, relieved to be able to move freely, sure by then that they were not being followed. They jogged single file, Lee in front,

Jennifer bringing up the rear. And when they came to a dip in the path where it veered sharply to the left, they didn't break stride.

And then the unthinkable happened.

Within the space of a few seconds, the three in front fell, Lee and Conrad tumbling far down the hill. Jennifer pulled up short just in time to see, around the side of two huge boulders, the green and glowing eyes of an alien.

It was going to leap onto Marysue, who lay winded on the ground immediately in front of Jennifer. For a moment Marysue was frozen, unable to move, but when she saw the sharp fangs of the creature bared for attack, she rallied enough to curl herself into a ball and begin a roll down the hill.

"Jen!" Lee called.

Jennifer ignored him and raised her club to wildly and erratically rain blows upon the creature's head, neck, and shoulders.

Surprised, it backed off. Then with a growl of rage it rushed at Jennifer.

She ducked and sidestepped, throwing herself on the undergrowth by the side of the path to roll down the hill to join the others.

Before she began to tumble, she took her club in two hands and smashed it onto the creature's foot.

And heard the satisfying crunch of bone and howl of pain.

When she stopped her free-falling descent, she looked back up the incline—the alien had disappeared into the cover of the woods.

"What on earth happened?" she asked the others, who had just struggled to their feet.

"The alien hid behind the rock and tripped me," Lee answered grimly. "And Zucco and Marysue were

following too close to stop. I couldn't see what it used—
it felt like a branch. But it was waiting for us all right."

"It must have been following us all along," Jennifer said
slowly. "With orders not to do anything unless we tried
to leave the woods."

"At least there was only one." Mary Sue was gingerly
unfolding and moving her arms and legs as if still uncer-
tain she was in one piece. "Any more and we would have
been done for."

"We will be, once the reinforcements arrive," said
Conrad. "Let's go."

They looked at one another, their faces drawn in the
late morning light.

And slowly jogged the rest of the way down the hill.

Two

THE VALLEY BELOW BALLAD HILL WAS NOT large. The small town of Staines ran down its center, and on the slopes of the hills surrounding it stretched pastureland and corn and alfalfa fields that, for the most part, supported dairy cattle. The only road leading in and out of town was two lanes. Once down out of the hills, houses began to appear on both sides of the road. They were old, usually made of white clapboards, which made them appear larger than they actually were.

Just before the town proper began was a house three stories high with a gray slate roof from which two chimneys poked. Dormer windows faced in all four directions. There was an open porch that ran around the house on all sides, keeping the first floor in constant shade. The front yard, small and neat, was rimmed by a waist-high hedge, in the center of which was a white picket gate. At the back the yard was deep, with a rock garden in the center, a metal toolshed to the right, a two-car garage on the left, and a low wire fence that separated the property from a wide field that now grew only weeds.

Marlene Chang stood in the dusk at her front door, wiping her hands on a dish towel. She wanted nothing more than to slam the door in the face of the fat man in a rumpled brown suit standing in front of her. He was

11

chewing on the end of a dead cigar, and though he hadn't insisted on coming in, she knew that he would if she hinted the offer.

"It's very important," he said earnestly.

"And I told you," she answered with a deliberately loud sigh, "that I don't know."

"It's important," he insisted.

She glared at him through the screen door. "What's important is that he be found, Detective Rumbel," she retorted. "This is the third day he's been gone, and none of you seems to be able to find *him* or the others."

"I know," he said apologetically. "But I have been trying."

Her look told him she doubted it.

A large truck growled down the road toward town, and he looked over his shoulder to follow its taillights until it was out of sight. Then he turned back and said, "Believe me, I don't want to arrest Conrad. I just want to talk to him. That's all. I swear it."

"You think he's a thief," she said coldly.

He hesitated before saying, "No. No, I don't."

Again the doubtful look. "And his friends?"

"I've just been to the Fawkes apartment," he said, suddenly eager. "They haven't seen their kid either. Mrs. Fawkes is worried to death. And I've asked them to do the same thing I'm asking you—please, when you hear from him, or any of his friends, give me a call right away."

"When he comes home," she said, "the first thing I'm going to do is tan his hide, then call the newspaper and let the whole town know how he's been hunted. Like a common criminal."

He looked up, looked side to side, and scratched at a jowly cheek that hadn't been shaved in several days. Then his shoulders sagged in defeat. "All right. All right."

He turned slowly and took the steps down to the flag-stone walk as if he were just barely able to carry his weight. He glanced around the yard, shook his head again, and walked through the gate to his car parked on the roadside. As he opened the door, he looked back at the house, and even at that distance his worried expression was clear.

Then he was in, and the car was gone, and Mrs. Chang closed the door thoughtfully.

She was a tall woman, her hair long and blond and curled into a loose bun at the nape of her neck. She wore a man's white shirt, jeans, and tennis shoes, and even those who knew her and knew how old her son was, would guess her age at a decade younger than she actually was.

Now, however, her face was creased with worry. She turned and crossed to the stairs, taking them two at a time. She turned right at the top of the second floor and hurried down the hall to a door at the far end.

She opened it and climbed a second, shorter flight of stairs that led into the attic.

"He's gone," she said, holding on to the metal railing that ringed the open stairwell. "You can come out now."

Jennifer, feeling like a little girl hiding from an angry neighbor, followed Conrad around the screen that separated the bedroom portion of the large room from the combination study and laboratory. Lee and Marysue were right behind, each with a sandwich in one hand and a can of soda in the other.

"Thanks, Mom," Conrad said, giving her a quick hug.

"I don't trust Rumbel," Lee muttered, walking to a large table covered with books and papers and sitting on the edge. "I just don't trust him."

They had been listening at the front window, Mrs. Chang speaking deliberately loud, thereby forcing the policeman to follow suit unconsciously. Jennifer wasn't sure what to make of it, but she could hear in the man's voice an uncharacteristic pleading and, she thought, a bit of fear too.

Mrs. Chang confirmed her impression. "He's afraid of something," she said. "I know him, and all that usual bluster of his is gone, believe me. He looks like he's seen a ghost." A wry smile crossed her face then. "Come to think of it, I guess from his point of view, he has."

"I still don't like it," said Lee. "A guy like that just doesn't change overnight."

"But it hasn't been overnight," Marysue reminded him. "He's had lots of time to think about it."

"Right. That's what I mean. Maybe he believed at first, but now I'm willing to bet he's convinced himself it was some kind of trick."

"At the moment," Mrs. Chang said, interrupting, "that's neither here nor there. What I want to know is, what you four are planning to do next."

Conrad immediately looked away and stared vacantly at a large globe beside him, which he spun idly with one finger.

Jennifer knew what he was thinking—whatever they did was going to be dangerous, and he didn't want his mother knowing anything in case the aliens, in their human disguises, attempted to contact her under the pretext of concern for her missing son. She might say something. She might, without knowing it, put herself in danger.

It had taken the four of them until late afternoon to reach Conrad's house, and they had spent an hour after that lying in the field observing the house. Watching. Listening. Looking for signs of surveillance and gathering their courage to make a run for the porch.

Finally, when the ground grew damp and hunger and exhaustion had overcome their caution, Conrad had run to the house. He had been inside so long Jennifer and the others became afraid. Finally he stood in the doorway and signaled them to come in.

Their first hour in the Chang house was tense almost beyond bearing. They all called their own parents and explained, briefly, that they were all right no matter what they might hear. Miraculously, all the questions they had expected hadn't been asked, and those that were had been put off with a simple, "Please, trust me, and I'll explain everything later."

And what was even more surprising was Mrs. Chang's willingness to believe them once they had told her the story of the aliens. She had sharp questions and demanded straight answers. When they had finished the questions, she said to her son, "All right, Zucco, what do you want me to do?"

And Jennifer, hearing her words, had nearly burst into tears.

"Now, look," Mrs. Chang said after sending Rumbel away. "You're not hiding anything from me, you know, Zucco."

He looked at her, and Jennifer wondered what he thought of his mother using a nickname that had been taken from an actor whose career was restricted to playing mad scientists. But then Jennifer remembered that it was his mother who had helped him equip the attic, encouraging all his interests, up to and including the occasional scientific experiment that, more than once, led to the house being filled with smoke.

She looked at them one by one. "I don't know," she said at last. "I have a feeling that if your father were alive he would approve of this, and that makes me nervous."

Conrad grinned and blushed faintly.

"I'm a mother, and that makes me a mind reader," she said with a smile. "I know you're going back there. It's written all over your face."

"Mrs. Chang," Lee began and stopped when she looked at him.

"You're going back," she repeated. "And you're going to try to get rid of them yourselves. Right?"

After a long moment Conrad nodded.

"Wrong."

Jennifer took a step forward. "But, Mrs. Chang, we don't have any choice!"

"Indeed you do, young lady," she said. "Before you go charging headlong into something that—that—." She stopped and cleared her throat. "What about your friends, that teacher and the librarian? Surely they ought to be of some help."

But the answer to that was obvious—the only other adults who had been on their side were Borden Overbrook and Pauline Klopher. Overbrook hadn't been seen since the night Jennifer and the others had fled into the woods. And Mrs. Klopher, who had divined the aliens' existence on her own and had discovered why they were here, had vanished before that.

Of course they could help, she thought with some bitterness, but no one knew where they were.

And she feared that Overbrook had been killed.

The muffled sound of the telephone ringing saved them from having to speak their fears aloud, and when Mrs. Chang had gone to answer it, Jennifer walked over to the window overlooking the road and put a finger to the pane. It was cold.

"What about Rumbel?" Conrad said. "Maybe we could—"

"Oh, sure," Lee said. "Show ourselves, and he'll have us locked up in a second."

In frustration Lee slapped a hand on the table, toppling his can of soda, and jumped down, cursing, while Conrad raced for an old towel to mop up the mess.

Jennifer waited until he was done, then boosted herself onto the wide sill and said, "I'm sorry, Zucco, but we have to do it, no matter what your mother says."

"I know," he said glumly.

"And we have to do it without her knowing it."

"How?" asked Marysue. "Tie her up and throw her in the closet?"

"If we have to," Lee said.

"Hey, I was only kidding."

"I wasn't," he said. "We can't wait any longer. We've got to go now, tonight, or it'll be too late."

"So what are we going to do?" Marysue asked sarcastically. "Walk up and knock on their door?

Excuse me, guys, but I'm here to stop you from taking over the world?"

"If we have to."

"Oh, for heaven's sake."

Jennifer barely listened to them bickering. The obvious plan would be to do just that. But they needed things they didn't have yet, such as weapons, a way to get in and out without being discovered, and a way to bring in the authorities without getting arrested.

That last had been her plan before, and it had almost worked.

Now, the chances of pulling it off were considerably less, and she wondered if she ought to be considering it at all.

Suddenly with a snap of her fingers, she pushed off the sill and said, "I know what to do."

Marysue looked at her skeptically, Lee with a scowl, Conrad with reluctant interest.

"Okay," Lee said when she didn't continue right away. "What's up your sleeve this time?"

"You'll love it," she said.

Marysue groaned and headed for the stairs. "That does it, folks. I'm giving myself up."

Jennifer took her arm as she passed. And smiled.

Beauford rolled her eyes. "This is gonna be trouble, right?"

"Right."

Lee finally broke into a grin. "Jennifer, you ought to be an actress, you know that? Or president. You sure know how to get our attention."

Jennifer let her smile fade. "Right after supper," she said, "we're going to get our ticket to the den."

Marysue looked puzzled as she turned to Conrad for an explanation, then abruptly turned back and said, "No!"

"Yes," Jennifer told her. "The moment we can get away, we're going back up to Thaler."

Three

THE MOMENT THEY WAITED FOR DIDN'T COME that night.

Mrs. Chang, well aware of what they were thinking, kept close tabs on them. There was no way they could leave without her knowing it.

Jennifer was growing increasingly impatient, however. Time, she knew, was running out—not only for them, but also for the rest of the world.

And when she thought of it that way, she nearly laughed. On the face of it, it sounded ridiculous, a melodrama that belonged only on a soap opera or in the worst science fiction film.

Which was virtually their whole problem—who in their right mind was going to believe that creatures from a distant star had been working on earth to transform its atmosphere into one only they could breathe, and no one else.

It was the stuff of children's bad dreams.

No matter that people had died since Jennifer had first made her discovery; no matter that she and her friends had destroyed one of the aliens' laboratories and located another one deep in the woods behind Ballad Hill; no matter that they had finally convinced a trio of adults that they weren't lying or making up stories.

19

It didn't matter, not when they were fugitives now from a law that would never listen to them; not when two of their adult allies were missing and possibly dead.

She stood to one side of the window overlooking Staines and watched the lights in the nearest houses, watched the far glow from the small business district. It isn't fair, she thought. Just because we're kids—it just isn't fair.

Lee walked up beside her, pushing an annoying thatch of sandy hair away from his brow. "Hey," he said quietly, "what are you looking at?"

She grinned at him. "Nothing."

He followed her gaze to Staines. "It looks so normal, doesn't it," he said.

"It's a dream," she answered. "Sometimes it seems like it's all a dream."

"Don't we all wish," he said, slipping his arm around her waist.

"We have to do it tomorrow," she said after a few minutes.

"I know. But how?"

"I'll think of something."

He smiled and shook his head. "As Beauford's always saying, it's your thinking, kid, that got us into this mess."

She put her arm around his waist and squeezed. He moved away from her after a few minutes. She didn't follow. Instead she sat on the sill and prayed to every god she had ever read about that somehow, in the morning, they would be given the chance to get up to the school.

Time; they had so little time left.

And the worst part of it was, none of them had an exact idea how short or long that period would be.

Even now it might be too late.

Thaler Academy sat in the cold, sharp morning light, behind a gateless brick wall on just over a hundred acres of ground on the high road that followed the contours of Ballad Hill. A broad, looping drive led to the main buildings, a crescent of seven that were two stories high and designed in the colonial tradition. To the right of the crescent were three Victorian homes, two of which were used by resident faculty, the third exclusively by the academy's dean.

From the woods opposite the entrance, Jennifer watched the activity on the campus for nearly an hour before she was convinced the police weren't there. There was no one stationed at the wall, no patrol cars that she could see. And when Lee returned from his reconnaissance of the grounds, he told her there were no cruisers in the parking lot either.

They waited fifteen minutes after Conrad's mother had gone before exiting the house by the back door, using the high weeds in the field behind as cover until they reached the hill. Then they made their way up the slope and hurried through the trees until they reached the school.

"You know," Conrad said then, "I have a feeling Rumbel didn't say anything."

Lee snorted in disgust and disbelief.

"No, I mean it, Lee," Conrad said. "If he still thought we were the guys he was looking for, wouldn't he have had the woods filled with cops? The way we were running, this way and that and not knowing where we were going, we would've been caught an hour after they started."

Lee looked away.

"And look at the campus. If they thought there was even a chance of our coming back, wouldn't there be someone there, watching?"

"How do we know there isn't?" Marysue asked.

After a moment's thought Conrad shrugged.

But Jennifer said nothing. She was concentrating on trying to make out the faces of the students, but it was almost impossible from that distance. A few she knew by their walks, a few by their garish or modish clothes, but the rest might as well have been wearing masks.

Then she grabbed Lee's arm, hard.

"Oh, no," Marysue whispered and crouched even lower behind the line of evergreen shrubs they had been using for cover.

From where they were, the Student Union was perfectly framed by the pillars at the start of the drive. And just coming out of the building was Peter Dramon.

Jennifer clasped her hands together to keep them from trembling.

Lee swore under his breath and said, "I wish I had a gun."

The dean, tall and handsome, was dressed in a black shirt and slacks that matched his dark hair. He stood out from the students like a beacon in the fog. He chatted with someone, nodded to someone else, and finally turned to his left to walk toward the administration building.

He did not once look down the drive toward the entrance, yet Jennifer couldn't help but feel that the man had seen them, and that if he pointed, every student on campus would come charging across the road to tear them to pieces.

Jennifer shuddered.

Lee stabbed at the ground with a stick.

They waited until the dean disappeared into the building, then Jennifer beckoned with a tilt of her head and they all moved to the left, staying below the level of the brush until they were past the academy entrance.

"You sure about this?" Marysue asked her then.

"Magic," she answered with a confident smile.

Cautiously, they edged down toward the road, and at Jennifer's signal pounded across it to dive into the trees and underbrush on the other side. At any minute they expected to be seen, to be captured.

Their breathing was harsh, their footsteps loud.

And when they reached the wall, they grinned in relief until Jennifer forced them on to a rusted iron gate. Beyond it was a stand of trees, a lawn, and the dormitory in which Jennifer and Marysue had their rooms.

Facing them, in the dorm's wall, was an iron fire door.

"Once we go through," Jennifer said, "we can't stop. We go in, check the hall, then immediately into my room." She fished a key out of her jeans pocket. "After that..."

But it was too late to worry about it. She pushed on the gate and closed her eyes when the hinges protested and the bottom scraped across the hard, worn ground.

Then she was through and making her way around the trees to the edge of the lawn.

She stopped and listened, waited until the others were behind her, then looked over her shoulder, took a deep breath, and said, "Now!"

It was the longest, most harrowing run she had ever made. Past the trees, out in the open, she just knew that a million eyes were watching her, a million lips grinning maliciously before screaming a warning.

And when she fell against the door, grabbed the handle, and yanked it open, she was so surprised she hesitated. Lee shoved her in quickly, making her stumble over the threshold.

A moment to catch her breath before she led them up the metal-tipped stairs to the second floor. The noises from the building were muffled in the stairwell, but she could tell as she approached the top landing that there were few girls inside right now. Many would be at lunch, a few still in classes. Where the rest were would depend on how well their luck held.

She waved to the others to wait, then opened the door a crack. Listening for voices, for music, or for a footstep.

Nothing. Nothing at all.

She poked her head out and checked the hall, looking front in case someone was coming up the center stairs, toward the back and at the door to her corner room. It seemed so far away, so terribly small, and she gripped the key so tightly it dug into the heel of her hand.

Jennifer slipped into the corridor and ran on her toes to the corner just opposite her door. A ball of lead fell suddenly into her stomach when she heard quiet voices in the shower room at the center of the hall.

There was no water running.

There was no laughter.

She waited several seconds, taking slow deep breaths, until she could wait no longer. Boldly, she stepped across the gap to the door, unlocked it, and shoved it aside. Closed the door and leaned against it, aware of the per-spiration that ran down her spine, aware of the trembling muscles that were refusing to keep her legs straight.

Then she straightened up, opened the door again, and with an eye toward the shower room, called once, quietly.

The others exploded from the landing and raced toward her, and she held the door wide until they all fell into the room. Then she shut it again, barely able to stop herself from slamming it. A turn of the lock, and she slid slowly to the floor, knees up, her forehead resting against them.

Jennifer looked up and around the room, mildly astonished that nothing had changed. It felt as if she had been gone for years instead of days, but the Sierra Club prints were still on the walls, her hairbrush and toilet articles still on the dresser, her books on the desk that faced the casement window.

"Step one," she said then.

"Right," said Lee, pushing his hands back through his hair. "So how do we accomplish the next one?"

The next one.

Jennifer stretched out her legs and leaned her head back against the door. "We check her room to see if she's in. If she is, we grab her. If she isn't, we wait until she gets back."

She was Monica Holt.

That night the last week on Ballad Hill an alien had warned them they had no place to go.

Unless the alien was a superb mimic, the voice they had all heard belonged to Monica.

All that time she had been one of them—an alien. All the assistance Monica had given Jennifer and her friends had been nothing but a way of keeping tabs on them. To learn what they were thinking. To find out what they were planning next.

The aliens had thus been one step ahead of them all the way, because of Monica.

The four students puzzled over why Monica had chosen to reveal herself at last and had finally found an answer. It was the aliens' only fault—their supreme confidence in themselves and their success had made them arrogant. After all, they had been on the planet for decades, and possibly centuries, conducting their genetic experiments with relative impunity. Anyone who might have stumbled over them had been killed or become convinced of the truth of legends about werewolves.

Arrogance.

And the closer to success they came, the more arrogant they grew.

They counted on fear and the unwitting participation of the police to help them remain hidden.

What they hadn't counted on was Jennifer's determination, Lee's anger, Conrad's horror, Marysue's strength. They hadn't counted on the fact that a bunch of kids wasn't going to surrender.

At least not without a fight.

"We can't wait any longer, you know. People will be coming back." Lee stood near the door. "And I can't be the one to go and check if Monica's in her room."

Jennifer looked hopefully at Marysue, who said, "We southern belles generally don't do very much sneaking around." The black-haired girl started buffing her nails on the curtains. "But I suppose I can make an exception this once." She started to stand, but Jennifer waved her back down.

"I might as well go. I want to stop in the shower room and freshen up anyway."

The corridor seemed silent, and Jennifer couldn't wait for a better moment. She eased the door open and started to slip silently down the corridor toward Monica's room. The sound of voices from the shower room had stopped, so Jennifer stepped inside there first.

She washed her face and hands before realizing she had no towel. The white plastic shower curtains were obviously unabsorbent, and there was no alternative but to dry her hands on her jeans. She shook off as much water as she could and rubbed the rest into the denim. She noticed that one of her shoelaces had come undone, and as she bent to tie it she saw just the lower part of a figure that limped into the room. Blue jeans and bare feet—and a bandage on one of those feet. The bandage had slipped slightly, just enough to reveal a tiny patch of fur.

Control, Jenny, she told herself. That's what you need right now. And she wondered how she would tell the others that she had found Monica.

And Jennifer straightened up and looked in the mirror at the face of the alien behind her. Not Monica's face at all.

Esther Fine's face.

Four

"SO YOU CAME BACK."

Jennifer almost didn't hear the alien speak, she was so caught up in trying to understand. Plain, hardworking, inconspicuous Esther, the timid student librarian. Esther had been one of them. She must have been the one who trapped Jennifer in the dark in the library, the one who kept her quiet, unnoticed eye on Mrs. Klopher, the one who tore up Pauline Klopher's room looking for the piece of evidence that had set Jennifer on the track of the secret lab—and the one who had attacked Jennifer and her friends a few days earlier.

"I heard you and Beauford didn't come home for the past four nights. Some of the rumors were pretty wild. What happened?"

Jennifer concentrated on looking Esther straight in the eye, on not looking at the foot that she herself had injured on Ballad Hill, on not letting Esther know that she had seen the fur beneath the bandage. "Oh, nothing as interesting as the rumors, I'm sure." She tried to edge around toward the door, to block Esther's escape until— until what? "We just stayed with some friends in town."

Esther was also moving toward the door. Had she guessed?

29

Jennifer felt the warmth of blood rushing to her cheeks. She lowered her head and her eyes fell directly to the bandage. Esther followed her gaze, looked back up and met Jennifer's eyes, and her manner changed. The wallflower disappeared, replaced by a coolly analytical alien.

"You can't do anything to stop us. We've got you now," she said. "What about the others? Are they in the dorm too?"

"No!"

Jennifer said it too quickly, too emphatically for it to be believable. She sidled again toward the door. She had to be able to escape. She had to warn the others so Esther wouldn't know where they were or what they were up to.

What could Jennifer do? If she could delay Esther long enough, Marysue might come looking to see what was going on, but that was a slender thread on which to hang her hopes. Keeping Esther occupied would be no problem, of course. That would be exactly what the mousy alien wanted. "I left the others at the Hilltop. You know, the diner in town?"

"Sure." The mask of innocence that Esther had worn so long was twisted by a smile. "They'll be safe there. It's a good thing you didn't bring the boys into the dorm. That'd be worth a trip to the dean's office for sure." Her round glasses glinted in the harsh light.

A cold chill crept up Jennifer's spine at the thought of being called into—trapped in—Dean Dramon's office. Esther was toying with her, but she had no way of striking back. No towels. Certainly no rope. No bathrobe sashes carelessly left behind. Nothing Jennifer could use to tie up Esther's arms and legs, even if she could overpower the alien.

Perhaps she could learn something, though.

"You must have been in charge of Mrs. Klopher. Taking care of her, I mean."

"The old biddy." Jennifer could sympathize with Esther's resentment. The librarian had dumped a lot of work on her assistant while researching the aliens. "She never even suspected that I was anything but a wimpy little freshman. She was surprised to run into me in the woods. Didn't even figure anything out until I shoved her into the tunnel," Esther gloated. She was enjoying this, reliving her triumph over the mere human who had dared to give her orders.

Mrs. Klopher was being held in the alien lab, or so Esther claimed. The woman had been captured after leading the others to the underground entrance behind the hill and had been held there ever since. Though Fine couldn't, or just wouldn't, explain fully, for some reason the woman fascinated the aliens. She was only a librarian, yet without the clues and evidence Jennifer and her friends had, she had managed to deduce the alien presence and, after a bit of snooping around, the ultimate goal of the experiments.

She was going to die.

Sooner or later, Pauline Klopher would die, but in the meantime, the aliens wanted to know more about her, how she thought, and if such thinking might help them.

Fine also claimed not to know anything about what had happened to Borden Overbrook. The ecology instructor hadn't been seen since the night of the fight in the clearing by Witch's Eye, the small lake where the final steps toward the lab's discovery had begun.

"Is it okay for you to tell me all this?" Jennifer asked, fascinated by the fluency and speed of the account.

"Sure." Esther was very relaxed about it. "Why not? I may have lost you in the woods, but now I know where you are, and you won't get away again. And, anyway, what can you do? You and your friends were on the loose for a few days, and who helped you? No one. So why shouldn't I tell you stuff if you can't do anything about it?"

Jennifer's maneuvering around the small shower room had done her no good. Each cautious half step to one side or the other was blocked, simply enough, by a parallel move by Esther. The two had moved a few feet closer to the door, so that Fine was almost touching it, but pushing Esther up against a closed door wouldn't get Jennifer out, and wouldn't protect Lee and Marysue and Conrad.

There didn't seem to be any way out of the shower room, unless Esther did something incredibly stupid, and that wasn't her style, Jennifer mused. But then all of a sudden Esther was catapulted across the space between them, arms flailing wildly, a wordless, panicky shout bursting from her lips. A step to the side, and Jennifer was clear. Fine hurtled past her to come up short beside the radiator. The alien doubled over the hot radiator for an instant, then stood up, whirled around, and glared back past Field to the door.

"Sorry, Esther," Marysue said. "I didn't know you were standing right there. Look, Field, we—we've got to get going, you know?" She gestured with her head in the direction of Monica's room.

"It's okay, Beauford. Esther knows."

"She knows? Oh, thank heavens. So you're in with us?" Marysue looked hopefully at the freshman.

"Look at her foot," Jennifer said. "She isn't on our side."

From that distance, Marysue couldn't tell anything except that there was a bandage on Esther's foot and, puzzled, she looked at Jennifer for some explanation.

"I saw fur under the bandage. She's one of them." Jennifer pulled down one of the shower curtains and started twisting it into a rope. "If she knows where we are and what we plan to do, she'll tell the others, and they'll come and stop us. We have to tie her up." She moved to her left and took a step toward the alien.

Marysue moved forward, too, blocking as much of the area as she could, bracing herself against Esther's certain dash for the door. "And we can't leave her here for someone to find. We need more time than that. Besides, that curtain won't hold her for long."

"Her room, then." Jennifer continued talking almost as though Esther weren't even there, stepping closer and closer, cornering the alien at the very back of the shower room. She passed one end of the twisted curtain to Marysue and they held it up like a barrier between them.

"It won't do you any good. I'll get loose, and I'll know where you are." Esther was getting ready, glancing from Jennifer to Marysue and back, and then suddenly she was on Marysue.

Beauford fell back with the surprise of the first blow, dropping her end of the curtain and stumbling against the row of sinks. Esther shoved her into the cold porcelain, but couldn't get past in time to keep from being grabbed by Marysue and swung around into the next sink.

Jennifer tried to wrap the shower curtain around Esther, but Fine and Beauford were grappling clumsily, pounding each other, although too close for the blows to have any serious effect. That same proximity made it impossible for Jennifer to tie up one without the other. And she couldn't wait for Marysue to get the upper hand because there was a strong possibility that that wasn't going to happen.

If only Jennifer could find a point of attack. Esther and Marysue were bouncing and spinning around the small room, and Jennifer could only follow them, waiting for them to settle into one position for just an instant, just long enough for Jennifer to grab Esther before she twisted around again.

And then the opportunity came as Marysue pulled away slightly, leading Esther into a shower stall.

In the instant that the alien prepared to pummel Beauford, Jennifer leaped forward and stomped on Esther's bandaged foot. When the alien reacted Jennifer was ready; she swept the alien's other foot off the slippery tiles, tumbling Esther to the floor.

Marysue rolled her over and sat on the small of Esther's back, pinning her down. Jennifer raised Esther's arms up and handed them to Marysue to hold while the curtain was fetched and twisted again. It was completely inadequate as a rope, but it would have to do until they could get Esther back into her room.

Once they had hauled her to her feet, it was an easy matter to keep Esther under control; Jennifer just kept one hand on her bound wrists and reminded the alien that if she made a fuss and anyone came running Marysue would rip off the plastic mask that made her look human. Marysue opened the door a crack to look around. "It's clear."

They hustled Esther back to her room and threw her on the bed. While Marysue held her down again, the shower curtain was replaced by one of her belts, and they tied another around her ankles and a scarf around her mouth. "This'll hold her," Jennifer said. "At least until we're long gone." As an afterthought, she took Fine's room key so they could lock up on the way out."

There was no more time to waste. They had to collect Lee and Conrad and get to Monica's room before she showed up.

When Marysue told the boys about Esther, they congratulated the girls on their resourcefulness, but Jennifer saw Lee give her a worried look.

"I know, I know, if Esther Fine, of all people, is an alien, then anyone could be. Anyone at all." Jennifer looked around at Monica's familiar room. Its normalness looked unreal. "That's why Monica has to lead us to the den today, as soon as possible."

Lee shrugged. "I don't like it, Jen. What if we can't get Monica to take us to the den? What if she won't do it? We're trapped."

Jennifer shook her head. "She will. I know it. How can she pass it up? We're the only ones besides Overbrook and Mrs. Klopher who know what's going on. She thinks we're stupid, she thinks we're helpless. She'll take us if only to prove how superior she is."

"And what," Lee said suddenly, "are we going to do when we get there?"

"Huh?"

"The den. Their lab. What are we going to do then?"

Jennifer had been waiting for the questions. "That is step two, part B."

Marysue narrowed her eyes. "Part B? You didn't say anything about a part B."

"I wasn't sure it would work," she admitted. "But I've been thinking about it, and now I'm positive it will. The next part depends on you and Conrad. At dinnertime you have to go over to the chem lab and—"

Marysue put her hands over her ears. I'm not listening," she said. "I don't want to hear it."

Conrad leaned forward, waiting for more details.

"Zucco," Jennifer said then, "when you get to the science building, you're going to need to find some things, and they've got to be rigged so that they're small and can be used quickly, without any preparation."

"What things?" Marysue asked, interested in spite of herself.

Jennifer told them.

Conrad, at first skeptical, suddenly grinned and applauded her silently, not wanting to attract the attention of the girls going by in the hall, and Marysue moaned comically about being too young to die. Then, abruptly, she was grim.

"Jenny, is this going to work?"

"I don't know. But right now I can't think of anything else."

"You know, Field," Lee said, "you're all right. You really are all right."

She felt a glow of warmth building in her cheeks and rubbed at them quickly. "Tell me that later. When it's over."

They waited for a couple of hours, and during that time Lee continued to glance shyly at Jennifer. One time when he looked up and smiled at her, she was so taken by it that she nearly missed what she'd been listening for all day.

She sat up, stood, and put her ear to the door.

The others froze.

Then she looked over her shoulder and nodded.

And looked away quickly because suddenly she was very, very afraid. Talking about walking into the enemy camp was one thing; talking about destroying it to prevent the atmospheric changes was one thing; talking about facing the wolf-creatures and defeating them was all talk.

But now, as she heard Monica Holt walking down the hall toward her room and laughing, she was going to have to do something about it.

The talking was over.

The time to act had begun.

Five

JENNIFER CLOSED HER EYES BRIEFLY AS LEE AND Conrad ducked behind her, pressing against the wall while Marysue leaped onto the bed and stood at the headboard. Then she pulled the door as slowly as she could until it was open about an inch. Monica's voice was clear now; she was talking with Barbara O'Malley.

Monica laughed, then she cursed when something fell with a thud onto the floor, and O'Malley moved on, giggling. Around the corner. Down the hall.

The sounds of frantic scrambling for spilled papers.

Jennifer peered through the opening and saw Monica on her hands and knees, trying to get an opened notebook back in order.

"Monica," Jennifer whispered.

Holt looked up, startled, then looked behind her as she slowly climbed to her feet.

"Monica."

Suspicion clouded her face, and she started to walk back toward the front of the building. Slowly.

"Monica."

She moved forward then and stared with narrowed eyes at the door to her own room.

Jennifer moved away from the door, her left hand still gripping the knob, her right bunched into a fist against her leg. Marysue had inched across the bed until she sat on the edge, only the night table between her and the door.

The squeak of a tennis shoe.

The distant sound of a radio being switched on.

Then Jennifer felt pressure against the door and moved back to let it open. Swallowing hard. Waiting until she saw the toe of Monica's tennis shoe poke into the room. Then she yanked the door to her, and Monica spilled in with a soft cry that was muffled when Lee and Conrad grabbed her and wrestled her instantly down to the bed.

The notebook dropped to the floor and sprung open again.

Jennifer closed and locked the door.

Marysue snatched up the lamp from the night table, yanked the cord from the wall socket, and held the lamp one-handed over her head, daring Monica to make a single wrong move.

But Monica, once her surprise was over, only relaxed and smiled.

"Well, well," she said smugly, "the little lambs have come back."

Conrad used his size and strength to keep her arms pinned behind her back as he roughly pulled her to a sitting position and got on his knees behind her. Lee went to the closet, opened it, and grabbed a cloth belt. With a look at Jennifer, he knelt in front of Monica and tied her feet together.

"I'll scream," Monica said.

Jennifer said nothing besides a crisp, weary warning to keep their voices down. Then, with a bitter sigh, she leaned against the dresser and stared at the girl she had once counted as a close friend.

Monica saw the look on her face and gave her a rueful smile. "Sorry, Field," she said. Then the smile turned mocking, and Holt's shoulders shook in a silent laugh.

Jennifer felt rage bubbling inside her.

With visible effort Marysue lowered her arm and returned the lamp to the table, crossed the room and pulled the desk chair to her, turned it around and sat, her arms folded across the back.

"So," she said blithely, "what's new in the galaxy?"

Monica gaped at her.

"Oh, give up, Holt. Playtime is over."

The alien seemed to sag in Conrad's grip, then recover and smile again. "For a moment you had me, Beauford."

"We still do."

Holt shook her head. "No. Not really. What are you going to do, throw me in the closet? Take me to the police?" She laughed harshly. "Right. Drag me all tied up down to the station and tell them I'm from outer space. When they want you to prove it, assuming they don't laugh you out of the place first, then what?"

Jennifer took two long steps to the bed, and before Monica could twist away, she reached down and pinched the alien's left cheek. And pulled as hard as she could until there was a faint, obscene tearing sound. Monica's mouth opened to scream, but Lee quickly clasped a hand over it.

And Jennifer stepped away in disgust, holding between her thumb and forefinger what looked like a limp strip of flesh-colored plastic.

On Monica's cheek there was a strip from just beneath her eye to just above her jaw—a strip of dark gray fur.

"No," she said. "I'll just pull off your face."

Without warning Monica began to struggle, lashing out wildly with her tied legs, whipping herself viciously from side to side and very nearly causing Conrad to lose his hold. Then Lee stood over her and calmly, silently slapped her twice against the skull.

The alien moaned softly.

And when Monica finally lifted her head again, whatever pretense to being human she had maintained was gone. The mutilated face was blank now, alien, the eyes dead and the mouth twisted in a smile of hatred.

"You'll pay," she warned. "You won't get away with this."

Jennifer laughed bitterly. "You sound just like someone in the movies."

The alien stared at the others. "You're all going to die. One by one. And I'm going to watch."

Lee pretended he was going to poke her side, and she flinched, but never lost the cold smile that twisted her lips.

"Okay," Jennifer said.

Monica stared at her. "What?"

"I said, okay. You want to see us die, then I guess we'll have to go and die, right?"

There was no comprehension, only suspicion, in the eyes that were drawn almost closed. "What are you talking about, Field?"

"Well," she said, "you can't kill us here, can you? So it stands to reason you're going to have to take us to the others." She paused. "To the lab, Holt. You're going to take us to the lab."

For a brief second only there was a look of triumph on the alien's face.

"Oh, no, you don't," she said. "Do you honestly think I'd take you there?"

"No," Conrad said gently from over her shoulder. "We know where it is. You don't have to lead us to it."

"Then what?"

"Just take us in."

"You're out of your minds!" she said.

"Look," Lee said harshly, leaning close to her ear, pressing one finger not too gently into her side, "I'm not like Jenny, and you know it. I can keep knocking this breathing patch of yours all day if you want. It won't bother me a bit. And sooner or later it's going to break down. It won't be able to turn our air into yours. And you know what? You'll suffocate. Like a fish out of water."

Then Lee backed off and dusted his hands against his jeans. "Jen," he said, "can you get something else we can use to tie her arms down? Zucco can't hold her all night. We have things to do."

She shook her head vigorously to rid it of the memory of Monica Holt as she had once been, went to Monica's closet and found several more belts, these of leather, which Conrad used to lash her arms together, and tie them to the bar of the footboard.

Monica, lying on her back with her feet toward the headboard, closed her eyes.

"Okay, Marysue," Jennifer said, "you and Conrad go to the lab. Now. It's dinnertime, and if you stick to the back, you ought to be able to get there without being seen."

Marysue clearly didn't want to stay in the same room with the alien. "Well, Zucco, let's get a move on."

Jennifer stood at the door, unlocked it, and listened until she thought the coast was clear.

She opened it.

Mentally crossed her fingers while she checked the hall and saw no one.

And almost before she was finished nodding, Conrad and Marysue were running toward the fire exit.

The door clanged behind them.

And on the bed, Monica suddenly exploded into laughter.

Jennifer whirled around, the door slamming as she did, and Lee again clamped his hand over the alien's mouth. She bit him, and he cursed loudly and told Jennifer to get him something he could jam into her mouth.

"Lee, what are—"

"You want them to come in?" he asked sharply, nodding toward the door.

A hesitation made him glare at her until she hurried to the dresser, grabbed a rolled-up pair of socks, and tossed it to him. He shifted his hand under Monica's jaw and squeezed until her mouth was forced open wide enough for him to jam the socks in. Then, with an explosive sigh, he sat back and examined his hand.

"I think she must be hungry," he said, holding the hand up for her to see the angry red teeth-marks across the fat of the heel. "We can't keep her here long, Jen."

"I know."

"And sooner or later someone's going to miss her."

"I know that too."

"Jenny—"

"For heaven's sake, Lee!" she exploded. "Will you please stop telling me the obvious? You think I don't know anything? Give me a break, huh?"

He said nothing; he only looked at her, his foot swinging slowly.

"Oh, Lee," she whispered. "I'm sorry."

"Just calm down a little, Jen, or you're going to fly right out the window."

And life in the dorm went on outside the door—bare feet running down the hall, someone shrieking, stereos blaring, groups of girls passing by, returning from dinner. Talking about their classes, their boyfriends, the teachers they wanted to string up. Giggling. A long stretch of swearing that made Jennifer blush and Lee break into a broad smile. Something made of glass breaking and an argument about whose fault it was.

Jennifer began to worry.

Lee began to fidget.

By her watch it was just over an hour since Conrad and Marysue had left for the science building, and though she knew that caution had to be observed, that they wouldn't be able simply to walk in and get what they needed, she still couldn't help thinking that the worst had happened— they had been caught. By the police or by Dean Dramon; she didn't know which would be the most disastrous.

More voices; more music.

She moved over to the window and looked down at the grass sweeping ahead of the dorm's shadow toward the first of the trees, looked to her right where the land sloped gently downward to the playing fields and the gymnasium. A number of girls in down ski jackets were walking here and there, and a group of them in warm-up suits was jogging across the field. The moon was already rising, pale and apparently transparent in the still-light sky.

Someone rapped on the door.

Lee instantly sat up, eyes wary and shifting, hands gripping the armrests. Jennifer moved as quietly as she could across the room, giving Monica a look and a warning touch to her side as she passed.

Jennifer listened, but there was no other sound—just someone walking along the hall, touching doors as she went by. The most innocent action was now marked with menace.

Marysue, she called silently. Where are you?

Her hands tightened into fists, relaxed, tightened again, and she knew she had to do something, anything. She could wait no longer. She walked over to the bed and sat on the edge.

"Lee, over there," she said and pointed to the other side of Holt's head. With a puzzled look he crossed over from the chair, and his eyes went wide when Jennifer pulled out the rolled socks.

Monica spat dryly and wrinkled her nose.

"Scream," Jennifer warned as her hand brushed the alien's side, "and you won't scream again." She held the rolled socks over the alien's mouth. "Not a sound."

Monica stared at her, looked at Lee as he sat on the other side of her, and finally nodded. "It won't make any difference anyway. I'm not going to be here long."

A voice in the corridor called out a name.

"How many of you are there?" Jennifer asked suddenly.

"What?" the alien asked incredulously. "You want me to say there are only five of us left? A dozen? Or would you feel better if I told you there were hundreds of us down there, prepared for war."

"Just thought I'd ask," she said blandly.

"Well, think again."

Someone rapped on the door, and this time they only exchanged indifferent glances, until the rapping came again and a voice—Esther Fine's voice—said, "Hey, Monica, you in there?"

Lee's hand moved swiftly to cover the alien's mouth before it could respond, and Jennifer watched, frozen, as the doorknob began turning.

Then a second voice asked what the problem was, and the answer was all too clear: "I'm looking for Holt. You seen her? The dean wants her, right away. Seems like one of her boyfriends got caught snooping around the labs."

Six

JENNIFER STARED AT THE DOOR IN HORROR AS THE two girls walked on, calling Holt's name until their voices faded.

The room filled with twilight.

Her throat was dry as she turned to Lee, who was stuffing the socks back into the alien's mouth.

Esther Fine had escaped, Zucco was caught, and they had no idea where Marysue was. If they didn't do something soon ... Jennifer shook her head sharply before her imagination got away. She had no time to panic; something had to be done.

Now.

And when Lee opened his mouth to speak, she held up a finger to silence him and moved quietly to the closet. Biting down on her lower lip, she scanned the inside until she found a final belt, then hurried over to the bed.

Lee looked questioningly at her.

She explained and they forced Monica into a kneeling position. They used the last belt to link wrists and ankles together, making it impossible for Holt to stand or to use her hands to free herself.

Then they dragged her to the closet and closed the door after they shoved her in.

"Wait," Lee whispered as Jennifer turned toward the door. "One more thing. Do you think she has a nail file? A metal one?"

She frowned at him, and when he gave her an insistent look, she rooted across the top of Monica's dresser until she found one. And watched in fascination as he leaned over the closet doorknob.

"What are you doing?"

"There's no doorknob on the inside," he grunted. "But I don't want to take any chances."

"Well, hurry!"

"Hey," he said. Then with a grin, he backed away—with the doorknob in his hand. "She'll have to be a magician to get out now."

Jennifer could only gape at him, finally smile, and they moved to the door and listened for movement on the other side. She didn't know exactly what they were going to do now, but she did know that her room was no longer safe. If Dramon had Conrad it wouldn't be long before he knew where they were, and they had to be gone when someone came over to check.

The moment there was a second of silence she opened the door and looked out. The hall was empty. Quickly she grabbed Lee, pulled him through, and locked the door. They ran for the fire exit and slammed out of it. She followed him down the stairs two steps at a time, her palm stinging as it slid over the banister, her lungs feeling as if they'd never get a decent breath.

Time, she told herself when she wanted to stop: there's no time, no time.

"Where?" Lee asked as they huddled at the exit.

"I don't know. He's either at the administration building, or in his house."

Lee mimed flipping a coin. "Administration," he said. "If he's not there..."

She put a hand on his arm as he reached for the release bar, silently begging him to wait, just for a second, just let her have a moment to think. His expression was filled with concern, and he hugged her close, pushed her gently away and let her know he understood.

But did he really? she wondered.

Lee Fawkes had had experiences she had never even dreamed about, knew things she thought were the exclusive property of those who lived outside the law. Did he really understand, then, that she'd never so much as stolen a piece of candy? That before she had come to Thaler she'd been so straight that she was often the target of good-natured teasing from her friends?

And now, as if living a nightmare, she was fighting for her life, using tactics she would never have thought herself capable of.

"Jenny," he whispered urgently.

She nodded. "Okay. I'm all right."

By his look he knew she was lying, but the only thing that mattered then was finding out about Zucco and Marysue; everything else took second place.

He leaned down on the bar and quietly eased the door open, and the early evening chill slipped into the stairwell. They could hear nothing and moved without delay, slipping around the building to their right until they were pressed against the back of the brick dorm.

There was still some light, but it was fading rapidly, slipping into the shadows that swelled in the trees less than a hundred yards away, touching the tops of the hills and making the slopes seem all the more dark by contrast.

They walked then, purposefully but without haste, keeping their heads down and their hands deep in their jacket pockets. If no one looked closely, they could have been any two students. Jennifer was counting on that. In the beginning she had been afraid that most of the student body was infiltrated by the aliens, but from the conversations in the hallway she decided she was wrong, especially when the mention of Dramon and one of Holt's "boyfriends" was done in the tones of simple gossip.

But that didn't mean there wasn't more than one.

So she kept her gaze focused on the tips of her feet, every so often flicking her eyes from side to side, checking the playing fields to their left, glancing up the breaks between buildings. And when they reached the structure that housed the administration offices, she looked around the corner on the first floor and saw that Dramon's room was dark. All his lights were out.

A look at Lee. He nodded that he'd noticed the same thing.

The temptation was to go right to the dean's house without checking. But they both knew the risk was too great, and they hurried around the side of the building. At the front they turned away from a group of passing joggers on the drive, too busy puffing and complaining to see them stride quickly to the steps and climb them.

Please, Jennifer thought as she pulled on one of the huge double doors.

It opened.

And they were inside before they had time to think.

The entrance hall was huge and made even larger by the expanse of white marble floor that reflected the dim glow of the huge crystal chandelier. The ceiling was high and elaborately bordered; the shadowy white walls were disected by dark beams and austere portraits of the academy's previous administrators. A fan-shaped staircase lay directly ahead of them, and the doors immediately left and right that led to secretaries' offices were closed and, as Lee discovered, solidly locked.

Beside the staircase was a hallway, and Jennifer hurried down it to a thick oak door beyond which she knew lay the dean's office.

The door was locked.

With a grimace of frustration, she rushed back to the center hall and joined Lee in a careful run up the stairs, holding her breath, fearing a squeaking step, glancing over her shoulder because she knew, she just knew someone was going to come through the door.

At the landing they stopped before continuing up the remaining stairs. On the second floor the high front windows were covered with thick draperies, and no light burned on the paneled walls.

They felt their way along the dark corridor, trying the doors. Again, as below, all were locked.

Until they reached the last one, and behind it heard the murmur of voices.

Jennifer's palm grew instantly moist, and she felt no better when Lee put a comforting hand on her shoulder. She pressed an ear to the heavy wooden door, but the voices were still muffled, and she shook her head, frustrated.

After an exchange of hand signals, Lee eased Jennifer to one side and ran his hands over the panels of the door until he found the old-fashioned glass knob and the oversize keyhole beneath. He crouched and squinted through the hole, and he signaled for her to wait before she crowded down beside him.

Several seconds passed.

Lee shifted to look through his other eye and tilted his head back to get a wider view; then he grinned and duck-walked backward to allow Jennifer to see.

The view she had of the room beyond was tunneled and blurred around the edges. But it looked like a study of some sort, with books on the far wall, a rich carpet on the floor, and a small, green-shaded table lamp to one side of a deep maroon chesterfield couch. On it sat Conrad, his hair in a tangle, his sheepskin coat pulled back and down off his shoulders to pin his arms at his sides. He was looking defiantly at someone sitting in a wing chair opposite him, but all Jennifer could see was a pair of crossed legs.

It was Peter Dramon.

She stared helplessly for what seemed like hours, watching Conrad's flushed face, seeing him occasionally struggle to free himself only to have an unseen person behind him push him down. Then he would slump back down in temporary defeat, though not once did his glare shift from the dean's face.

Lee pulled at her shoulder.

She shrugged him off.

He tugged again and finally she eased away and moved silently away with him to the center of the hall.

"We have to do something!" she whispered in his ear.

He nodded, agreeing, then shrugged his shoulders. What could they do? Even if the door wasn't locked, they couldn't charge in. They had no weapons. Those inside might. And there was still, he reminded her, the problem of Marysue—they had no idea if she was in the room or hiding someplace.

He shrugged again—a stalemate.

She refused to believe there was nothing they could do and she stared at the door while her mind raced through absurd and impossible plans. Suddenly she brightened.

Taking Lee's arm, she led him back to the staircase and a few steps down.

"What?" he asked.

"I'm going in there."

"You're what?" And he looked up to the hall, his voice sounding to Jennifer like a shout. "What are you talking about?"

"I'm going in," she said. "If the door's open, I'll just walk in. If it's locked, I'll knock. But I'll go in."

"Great. And what good will that do?"

"He's not tied up," she said. "Which means he can run if he gets the chance. But he hasn't had the chance because whoever's behind him is either bigger, stronger—"

"Or has a gun or something," he grumbled.

"Possibly."

"Possibly? C'mon, Jen, this is crazy. You can't go in there alone."

She smiled at him. "I know. I'm not."

He looked at her, puzzled, trying to read her mind, and when she finally told him what she was thinking, the first thing he did was take a step down and tell her she was only asking to get them all killed. Then, because she said nothing and only looked at him patiently, he walked back to her and took her hands, telling her she was being silly, that they needed more help. She responded only with silence. He understood then that their help was the only help Conrad was going to get.

He looked away from her, at her, and away again.

She tugged at his hands.

He scowled at her for a second before planting a solid kiss on her cheek. "You *are* nuts, you know."

"Me? I'm scared to death."

"Good. That makes two of us. So let's get it over with before one of us chickens out."

She felt no relief, yet the fear that had ridden with her since they had left the dorm was less menacing somehow, less sharp, and she preceded him down the hall and to the door, taking hold of the knob.

"Remember," she whispered.

His nod was abrupt.

And with a deep breath she turned the knob, pushed the door inward, and stepped over the threshold.

Seven

THE TABLEAU JENNIFER FACED MIGHT HAVE BEEN funny had she not gone cold with fear the moment she stepped into the room, her hand still on the doorknob.

Peter Dramon had risen from his chair and was staring at her, first in amazement and then with just a hint of admiration for her courage. A slow and feral smile broke across his face. Conrad was startled and gaped at her before renewing his struggles to pull his arms from the sleeves. For his efforts he was rewarded by a vicious slap across the back of his head by the person standing behind him.

"Hello, Barbara," said Jennifer tightly.

Barbara O'Malley, wearing an old gray sweatshirt with the sleeves rolled up and faded jeans that were worn through at the knees, grinned maliciously at her. "Field," she said, running a hand through her curly red hair, "I was wondering when you'd figure it out."

"Be careful, Jenny," Conrad warned. "They don't know anything."

O'Malley lifted her hand to slap him again, but he sensed the blow and flinched, frustrated and furious at his helplessness.

Jennifer, despite everything telling her to turn and run for her life, stood and scanned the large room swiftly. She saw no one else. And other than a narrow sideboard with wine glasses and a tall decanter beside the door, she could see only a few pieces of elegant furniture, back in the shadows where the feeble light from the lamp failed to reach. The high arched windows, like those in the hall, were completely covered by drawn wine velvet drapes.

Dramon recovered quickly and, as if he were in the company of old friends, nodded and casually slipped his hands into his pockets. "Miss Field," he said genially, taking a step toward her, "I'm very pleased to see you. May I assume this unexpected visit is some sort of last-second rescue mission for your not-so-little friend here?"

Jennifer took a hesitant step to her right, away from him, and asked Conrad if he was okay.

Zucco's broad smile was full of bravado, though his eyes betrayed the fright he'd been given. "I guess I was pretty clumsy," he confessed. "I got in okay, but then I knocked over a stupid trash can in the hall, and this one"—and he nodded back toward O'Malley—"saw me before I could find a place to hide. The next thing I knew I was up here."

Dramon grunted.

Jennifer carefully kept her expression blank, realizing at once that he was deliberately keeping Marysue's name out of his explanation. "It's okay," she said quietly. "As long as you're not hurt."

"Not yet," Barbara said flatly. "Now why don't you just come over here, Field, and let's get on with it. I'm tired of wasting time when I have better things to do."

"What things?" she asked.

O'Malley shook her head. "Sorry, Field. Now why don't you just—"

"In a moment," Dramon told her sharply. "I want to know where the rest of them are." He moved another step closer, trying to herd her away from the door. "And I think, Miss Field, there had better not be any more lies. This young man has told enough to last quite some time."

She backed away until she felt the carved rim of the sideboard press against her thighs. A decent breath was hard for her to come by, and what air she did manage to pull into her lungs was laced with a chill that raised gooseflesh on her arms.

Dramon stopped. Half in shadow, half in light. His eyes had grown even darker, and the widow's peak formed by the backward sweep of his black hair gave him a satanic look. But it was his voice that terrified her—cold and flat, each word, though softly spoken, made her react as if she had been slapped.

"Miss Field, I'm waiting," he said, making it clear his patience was at an end. He looked at O'Malley and she reached forward suddenly and grabbed Conrad by the hair, yanking back his head until his neck and back were arched. "I am not averse to inflicting a little pain, Miss Field, as you can see. And Miss O'Malley here has shown me she is quite efficient with the side of her hand."

O'Malley grinned and with a cruel flourish touched the center of Conrad's throat with her hand, then lifted her arm and held it in a striking position while she continued to pull back slowly on his hair. His face reddened, his eyes closed tightly, and he began to grunt with the double effort of trying to breathe and stave off pain.

Jennifer put a hand over her stomach and looked away from the scene, only to see the alien's shadow on the far wall—arm up, hand flat, and Conrad's head back as though he were lying over a guillotine's block.

"If she should hit him just right," Dramon said as if delivering a lecture, "there's no question but that he would suffocate." His eyes narrowed even further. "Well, Miss Field?"

There was no chance, she thought. If she tried to grab Barbara or if Lee decided to make his charge then, that hand would slam into Conrad's throat before either of them had taken a single step.

She had no doubt the man was telling the truth—one blow and Conrad would be dead.

Dramon had moved directly to her left then, his hand resting lightly on the doorknob, a single long look into the hallway evidently allaying whatever suspicions he might have had that she hadn't come alone.

Jennifer held her breath, wondering where Lee had gone.

"I'm waiting, Miss Field," he said with exaggerated patience.

"Are you one of them?" she asked suddenly, turning to face him, bracing herself hard against the sideboard and causing the glasses to tremble.

Dramon only smiled. "The questions, my dear, are mine tonight. Don't think I don't know you're stalling. Perhaps waiting for the other two to arrive? Perhaps the police?" He shook his head then. "No, I don't think so. The police aren't exactly your friends these days, are they?"

As he moved away from the door toward her, he pushed it closed lightly and—Jennifer noted with a brief prayer of thanks—apparently didn't realize that the latch hadn't caught.

Barbara growled low in her throat.

"You have ten seconds, my dear," the dean told her. "Ten seconds to tell me where I can find the others, or your number will quite dramatically be cut down to three. And then, just as quickly, two."

Jennifer pressed her right hand harder against her stomach.

"One," Dramon said and smiled gently at her.

"I don't know," she blurted out. "Honestly, I don't know."

"Two."

"We were supposed to do different things," she said in a pleading tone, her gaze darting from side to side as he continued to count. "Honestly, I'm telling you the truth! We all had different things to do. I don't *know* where Lee and Marysue are!"

"Five," Dramon said, folding his arms over his chest and leaning against the wall.

Conrad, his eyes open now and staring at the ceiling, began pushing back with his feet planted squarely on the floor, but O'Malley didn't relinquish her grip on his hair, nor did her arm waver. She only looked over her shoulder at Jennifer and stared, waiting.

Jennifer began trembling. "Mr. Dramon, please, don't hurt him. I swear I'm telling the truth. Don't you think if I knew where they were I'd have waited for them or gone to get them before I came in here?"

"Nine," the dean said.

"You said I was smart," she said, nearly shouting. "You think this is smart?"

O'Malley raised herself up slightly on her toes, expecting the order to be given. She only frowned when the dean said to her, 'Ten, and wait just a moment, my dear. Your time will come."

Jennifer sagged against the table.

The dean pushed off the wall and lowered his head. "What do you think, Barbara? Does she lie that well?"

Barbara's face had taken on an expression of hatred and hunger, and her only response was to snarl and pull on Conrad's extended neck. But Jennifer saw what Barbara hadn't—that the farther he was forced to lean back into the couch, the more he was able to pull his arms out of the sleeves; an inch or so more and his elbows would be free, and once that was done he'd be able to pull them out completely.

Suddenly she had a thought and no time to decide if it would work or not.

"Let him go," she said to the dean. "And I'll tell you where Monica is."

Her relief was almost palpable when Dramon took a half step back and Barbara lowered her arm slightly. The reaction was a confirmation of something she had already concluded that afternoon—that Monica wasn't simply a guard, she was far more important. If not on an exact level, then probably not too far below Dramon in the hierarchy they had.

"You are bluffing," Dramon said then.

"No," she answered. "And if you don't cooperate, she'll be in as much trouble as Zucco is now."

"Liar!" O'Malley spit.

Jennifer shrugged. "Maybe. Maybe not. It's your move."

Dramon drew a thoughtful hand over his mouth, glancing at the boy on the couch and looking at Barbara, who was buying none of it and said so with a sneer. Jennifer didn't care, as long as she was able to keep them inactive for another minute or two.

"Nonsense," Dramon finally said. "Miss O'Malley, if you please." And he nodded.

And Jennifer swept the array of glasses off the sideboard with a stiffened arm, causing Dramon to leap out of the way. In the same motion she snatched up the decanter, whirled, and threw it spinning at Barbara, who had been startled enough to freeze just before the heavy faceted glass struck her on the temple and drove her groaning to the floor.

Conrad instantly rolled off the couch and onto the floor, and Jennifer raced around the back of the couch, leaping over the barely conscious Barbara and knocking the lamp off the table. When it struck the floor, it sparked and went out, and the room was plunged into a darkness relieved only by a sliver of light falling between the heavy drapes.

Dramon snarled. "A foolish move, Miss Field," he said. "A very foolish move."

Although she was temporarily blinded by the darkness, Jennifer did find Conrad, who was crawling away from the couch, and helped him to his feet. Then she grabbed his elbow and guided him back to where Barbara was struggling to her hands and knees behind the couch.

"A foolish move indeed," Dramon said.

She couldn't see him.

There was only the faint spill of light and no more.

But she could hear him—moving stealthily across the carpet, making little attempt to be silent. His breathing was deep and steady, and when he clapped once, sharply, she couldn't stop herself from uttering a short scream.

"He's trying to scare us," Conrad said from behind her.

No, she thought. He's letting us make all the noise so he'll know where we are.

Another clap.

Barbara moaned, and Jennifer, though she couldn't see him, felt Conrad lean down. There was a muffled thud, and the sound of something dropping heavily to the floor.

"What a waste of time," Dramon said.

Jennifer started—he was closer, on her right.

She backed away, sidling toward the door, using her left hand to guide herself along the couch and hoping Conrad was following.

"A pity," said the dean.

She blinked—now he was on her left, somewhere between her and the hall.

A trick. It had to be a trick. He couldn't be two places at once.

"This is one time, girl, you're not going to get away."

Behind her.

She whirled around, hands up to defend herself, and swayed because the quick movement in the dark made her dizzy.

Conrad! Where was Conrad?

"You asked me a question before, girl."

She whirled around again.

"I think you deserve an answer."

And a strong, cold hand closed around her neck.

Eight

AIR, JENNIFER THOUGHT IN DESPERATION AS SHE grabbed for the hand. Air, I need air.

Frantically she lashed back with her heels while trying to twist out of the man's grip. But she felt herself being lifted effortlessly off the floor and lashed out again. Her foot struck something, but there wasn't so much as a grunt or the slightest easing of the pressure around her throat.

Higher, lifted higher, and the scream that exploded from her lungs came out as a whimper.

Her chest burned.

The dark became speckled with flecks of red and slow spinning gold.

Her kicks became more feeble, her throat laced with fire, and her arms turned wooden, and she slowly lowered them to her sides.

Then she heard through the roaring in her ears a shattering of glass and a groan, and the hand that held her was gone. She slumped to the floor and lay on her back, fingers pulling at her throat in an effort to widen the passage and let in the air. Then she was up again, floating, flying, and the dark lost its colors and lightened.

"What took you so long?" She barely recognized her own voice rising above the roar of the blood in her ears. "I thought we'd had it for sure."

Another voice answered, but she couldn't understand it, a low voice, a familiar one, and her eyes fluttered open to see Lee's hard-lined face just above hers.

Floating.

The dark driven into shadows as she was carried down the stairs.

"I'm all right," she gasped weakly.

"Sure you are," he answered softly, not looking at her, concentrating on taking the stairs down to the hall. Then, to Conrad, "What happened?"

"It's just like I said—that damned redhead saw me as I was going into the lab. I knocked over that trash can to warn Marysue and then O'Malley was there with a couple of her ugly friends."

"You let them beat you?"

"Marysue was already inside. I didn't want them to know."

In the downstairs hall at last, Lee lowered Jennifer gently to her feet. She clung to him gratefully, laying her cheek against his chest until her lungs could work without protest, until her vision cleared and she saw where they were.

A hand lifted her chin. "Are you okay, Jen?"

A nod was all she could manage, but it satisfied him and he grinned, then looked anxiously back at the staircase and said, "We can't stay here. C'mon."

Conrad opened the door a crack, peered out, and beckoned. They hurried without running, moving down the stairs and to their left, ducking into the gap between buildings, not stopping until they reached the back corner. There they fell against the wall for a moment's rest.

It was nearly dark.

The white globes spaced along the drive glowed with a faint halo, and when Jennifer looked up she could see the stars beginning to break up the sky. Her fingers massaged her throat tenderly while the other hand pressed against her chest. Her breathing was easier, but she couldn't shake the feeling that a hand was still back there, somewhere behind her, just waiting to return to her throat.

"Marysue," she said and coughed.

Conrad told her not to worry, touched Lee's arm, and whispered something to him. Then he was gone, and Lee was tugging lightly at her hand.

"Can you run?"

"Away from them? Any time."

A quiet good-luck wish to each other, and they broke from the protection of the building and raced across the back lawn to the woods, nearly stumbling even though the slope was gentle, not stopping until they had reached the shadows under the trees. That they hadn't been spotted was a minor bit of luck.

The warning would go out as soon as Dramon came to his senses.

They were the hunted then, instead of the hunters.

Taking care to make as little noise as possible, they moved through the trees and underbrush parallelling the buildings on their left, freezing each time a light flared on in a dormitory room, ducking every time they saw a student moving across the campus. They knew they couldn't be seen, yet they felt as if they were completely exposed, a spotlight marking their every step.

When they reached the last dorm, they drifted farther back into the woods and stopped.

And Lee said, "I'm sorry, Jen."

"It's all right," she told him with a smile.

"I didn't realize the door opened inward. I knew he'd look out so I had to get back to the stairs and hide there."

"Lee, it's okay."

"You—you could have been killed."

She laid a palm against his chest. "No," she said. "I had my knight in shining denim."

He looked at her for a long time before looking away. "That," he said, "is the corniest thing I've ever heard in my life."

She laughed silently. That was Lee through and through. He seldom permitted his emotions to break through the tough-guy role he usually acted.

"I have to get Monica," he said then, nodding toward Jennifer's window on the second floor.

She almost panicked. "You can't go in there now, Lee. If someone sees you—"

"They already have, right, so what more do we have to lose now? Besides, we can't leave her there. We have to get her before Dramon finds out where she is."

"All right," she said, not liking it a bit. "But please don't do anything stupid."

"Who? Me?"

"Lee," she warned.

"All right. No heroics. I swear."

She gave him the key then and told him she'd wait until he signaled her by turning on a light in her room— once, twice, once. Then she would make her way through the woods to the trees opposite the fire exit. "Be careful," she added, kissing him on the cheek. She shoved her hands into her coat pockets as she watched him waste no time moving.

And as soon as he disappeared around the corner she tried to follow his progress by picturing him moving up the stairs—probably two at a time—listening at the landing door, testing to see if it was locked before opening it, running down the hall to unlock her door, and going in.

A look at the window.

Darkness.

Maybe someone was in the hall, she thought, and he had to wait. She gave him thirty seconds in a slow count, and thirty more just in case.

The window remained dark.

She shifted her weight from foot to foot, trying to ignore the sharp chill, the rustle of the leaves over her head, the woodsounds behind her. Things moving, creeping, snapping twigs and rustling branches. She held aside a drooping bare branch and looked down toward the administration building, but it was hidden by the curve of the crescent, and she bit down on the inside of her cheek, worrying about Conrad and Marysue.

She hunched her shoulders and pressed her arms tightly to her sides.

A light snapped on, and she started to move, but stopped and cursed when she realized it was the wrong room. A shadow against the drawn shade. Another joined it. The creak of a hinge as the window opened and music drifted softly into the night.

She began easing to her right, always keeping her room in view. The idea that Lee might be in trouble was difficult to combat, and she had to restrain herself from breaking into the open to find out what had happened.

He's all right, she told herself. He's all right.

The music blared for a second before being turned down.

She thought about Barbara O'Malley; she thought about Dramon and wondered what the answer to her question would have been—was he an alien? Had he really intended to kill her?

From the far side of the dorm came an explosion of high laughter, a shriek, another laugh.

"Lee, where are you?" she whispered urgently.

She considered moving into place opposite the fire door and changed her mind. She wouldn't be able to see her window from there, and she needed to know Lee was all right.

He isn't, a small voice told her then.

She stiffened.

He's in trouble. He needs you.

Again she felt panic threatening to rise. Too much time had passed, and they had no time. She had to do something, now, before it was too late. She never should have let him go on his own. She should have gone with him.

She stepped out of the woods and started up the slope, and froze when the light went on in her window.

Once.

Twice.

Once.

And then it was dark.

She was so relieved she wanted to shout; she looked up to the sky in gratitude, then ran back to the trees, not going in but keeping inside their shadows until she reached the pines that faced the building's side. Ducking behind a large trunk, she stared at the door, willing it to open, demanding that Lee appear. Now!

And he did.

Staggering across the grass with a bundle over his shoulder. She hissed his name when he was near enough to hear, and he swerved toward her so sharply he nearly stumbled. She grabbed the trunk so tightly she thought she would crush it. She stepped away when he joined her and lowered his bundle to the ground.

It was Monica, unconscious, and the roll of socks was still crammed in her mouth.

Lee bent over, hands on his knees, mouth open as he worked to control his breathing. Then he looked at her sideways and grinned. "Do you have any idea how many naked women run around that place at night?"

She slapped his shoulder, and he laughed and straightened up with his hands on his hips. Then he shook himself as if that were enough to bring back his strength.

"Let's go," he said, reaching down, and with Jennifer's help, hung the alien back over his shoulder.

"What about Conrad?" she asked as they headed for the gate through the woods.

"He's gonna meet us, don't worry."

"Where?"

"Outside."

And once through the gate they moved quickly to their left, dropping Holt back to the ground.

"Lee," she said, pulling him away from the alien, who was beginning to groan as consciousness returned. "Lee, I have an idea."

He looked at her, his face red from his exertions.

"If we could get her into Staines," she said, pointing at Holt, "we wouldn't have to go to the den! I'm so stupid, I didn't think. We have all the proof we need at last. Right here. Right there!"

The headlights of a car began to sweep over the wall that surrounded the school, and they dropped to the ground until it passed.

Without the lights the night seemed much darker.

Lee pushed himself to a kneeling position. "You want me to carry that thing all the way into town?"

"There are four of us, remember, Lee? And she doesn't have to be carried, for crying out loud. She can walk. She can't get away."

Still breathing hard, he looked from Holt to Jennifer and let himself smile. "No commando raids?"

"We won't need to."

"Y'know, Field, I think you've just saved my life."

She smiled, but felt little relief. The idea was so obvious she wondered why she hadn't thought of it before. So much going on, so many fears to conquer—and everything they'd been trying for was literally lying at their feet.

"What about Dramon?" he asked suddenly.

"Yes," said a voice from the dark by the wall. "What about me?"

Nine

JENNIFER COULDN'T BLOCK A SHORT, SHRILL scream as she stumbled backward when the man stepped away from the wall.

Lee reacted more swiftly, spinning as he leaped to his feet, a fist already up and his face creased with rage. But Dramon easily sidestepped the clumsily aimed blow and with a contemptuous snarl delivered one of his own—an almost languid sweep of his arm that knocked Lee off his feet and into the brush.

"Jenny, run!" he shouted, and after a moment's fearful indecision, she did, leaping over Monica Holt's prone figure into the open where she raced along the wall toward the campus entrance. Dramon was right behind her; she could hear his footsteps, could almost feel him reaching for her shoulder.

She veered sharply and leaped onto the road, arms pumping, eyes straight ahead. She glanced into the main entrance of the school when she passed it by, hoping that either Conrad or Marysue would be waiting there with a miracle to save her. But the drive was empty, and no one came running toward her over the lawn.

After another few feet she looked back to see how close Dramon was, how near she was to being captured.

And she slowed.

Dramon wasn't there.

She stopped, panting, and saw him in the shadow of the wall, bending over Holt and working to loosen her bonds. Then she saw a figure break from the trees—Lee—and sprint, limping slightly, across the road. He slid down into the shallow ditch beyond the shoulder and then clambered up into the woods.

Dramon stood then, hands on his hips, while Holt struggled to kneel in front of him.

Jennifer stared back, deliberately making a show of pushing her hair out of her eyes, thinking that if she was able to keep the man's attention long enough Lee would be able to put distance between him and the aliens. But when the dean took a long step toward her, she bolted and crossed the road and dove into the woods without looking to see if he had followed.

With a forearm up to prevent branches and twigs from scouring her face, she used her other hand to pull herself up the hillside. She made no attempt to be silent; the panic she had been fighting all day had finally surfaced, had finally taken over, numbing her mind and burying her judgment.

She ran, fell, ran on again, blindly. Not checking her direction, not looking behind her. Instinct was the only thing that moved her now. The instinct to put as much distance between herself and Dramon as she could.

Her mouth fell open as she gulped for air. Her ankles turned over dangerously when she stepped and stumbled over night-hidden rocks and fallen limbs. She tripped over something, sprawled face first onto the ground, quickly rolled over, and scrambled to her feet again.

He's coming, she thought.

Lee, where are you?

And she ran faster, dodging around trees that suddenly grew in her path, using their trunks to thrust herself onward, upward, until finally her legs could take no more punishment, her lungs were incapable of drawing in the necessary air.

She fell in stages, first to her knees, then to her hands, and then, when not even her arms had the strength to support her, onto her chest.

The blood roared in her ears, and behind it began a faint buzzing that made her dizzy. Her stomach roiled with acid, and her muscles were threatening to cramp.

Up, she told herself. Get up, he's coming.

Lee!

Swaying drunkenly, she staggered to her feet and stumbled forward a couple of steps before falling again.

And again she cursed herself, tears falling freely onto her cheeks. One step, and another, and then she was able to put two together without losing her balance, then three, then four, and though she wasn't running, she was moving.

Coming. He's coming.

Her shoulder scraped against a tree trunk.

Her shin cracked against an outcropping of rock.

Lee, please help me!

The angle of the slope kept changing—steep for a few yards, flat for a few yards more. Every so often it suddenly dipped downward, nearly spilling her over. Rivulets of perspiration stung her eyes, and she wiped a sleeve over them angrily. A thorn snagged the bottom of her coat, and she yanked at it, sobbing out loud, until she was free.

Lee, she thought then. Lee? Where is Lee?

She stopped and held her palms to the sides of her head, trying to think, forcing herself to think. At last she began to move more slowly as she expended her second wind and the aches in her legs and arms became too great to ignore.

Staggering until her knees wobbled and gave out.

Falling, and not caring. It was good not to be moving, and she didn't care if Dramon did catch her, if Holt had awakened and had joined in the chase. She didn't care. Her legs hurt. Her side hurt. The perspiration was cold on her skin, and she was shivering uncontrollably, so much so that she curled into a tight ball and willed the world to go away.

Lee.

Her teeth chattered.

Lee. And Marysue.

Her eyes opened, closed, opened.

Conrad.

Where were they?

And at last she could feel the panic receding, a tide turning to let her think again clearly.

A soft moan, a softer whimper.

Then she gave herself to the count of one hundred before testing her legs by straightening them. She grimaced in anticipation of cramping and expelled a loud breath when there was none. She hauled herself to her feet and started moving again in the direction Lee had taken, hoping their paths would cross, praying he hadn't decided to go back to the road.

And when the panic was finally gone and she felt herself back in control, she realized that her night vision did allow her to see more than she had thought. And she was able to hear again— the leaves, a soft breeze, and the distant hum of an automobile racing along the road below.

Her lips parted to call Lee's name, but she caught herself in time. Instead she continued on, straining to hear something to indicate that he was moving as well. She would mark his direction and follow it. Sliding into a hollow and climbing out again, swearing at the crackling of the leaves underfoot and knowing there was nothing she could do to silence them. Grabbing onto a slender trunk and leaning forward, wishing for a signal, demanding one, blinking away an abrupt rush of fear when she realized she had been staring blindly at the lights of Thaler, down through the trees.

A few deliberate breaths, and she moved on. Taking the slope closer to the road but always heading in Lee's direction. Swallowing hard and moistening her lips, she froze when she thought she heard voices. The wind, she thought then. It's just the wind.

The temperature seemed to fall.

She ducked, climbed, several times finding a lane clear enough for her to run a few yards.

Downward, until she was directly opposite the place where Dramon had knocked Lee down. By raising herself up on her toes she was able to see that the spot was empty: Holt and the dean were gone. Instantly she dropped into a crouch and listened, but heard nothing. Then she rose slowly, squeezing her eyes shut when one of her knees cracked so loudly she was sure it had been heard all the way down to Staines. She inched to her left and carefully pushed an evergreen branch aside.

A clear view straight down.

Nothing.

And no sound.

She was in approximately the spot where Lee had vanished into the trees, and there was no sign of him now.

He had obviously done as she had—run away from the danger as fast as he could.

Now she had to make a decision, and make it soon. Staying there was foolhardy. It wouldn't take long for Dramon to get his people organized into a search party, if he hadn't done so already, and she needed to be as far away from Thaler as she could before that happened.

But where could she go?

Double back onto the campus in the hope that they wouldn't think she'd try such a thing? Or should she head down into the valley, to Conrad's house, and try to enlist the help of his mother?

She tried to imagine what Lee would do. He had been limping slightly when she last saw him. Would he think she would head for Witch's Eye and try to meet her there, or would he take the safest route, down to the Changs? There was no sense trying to think about Mary-sue and Conrad—Lee hadn't told her what he and Zucco had planned except that they were all going to meet outside.

Well, she was outside, and there was no sign of them; they might have heard the commotion and already fled.

But, where?

Then she heard it.

Behind and above her, from the crest of Ballad Hill.

The low, soft howling of a wolf.

All choice was taken from her, and she abandoned caution as fear drove her from her cover. She thrashed her way straight down to the road, breaking into an all-out run until she remembered the distance she would have to travel. It was three miles to Staines, but she couldn't go back to the campus, and she couldn't move nearly so fast in the woods.

So she ran, but held herself back from sprinting. Conserving as much energy as she could.

Her footsteps loud and sharp.

Her breath began to fog in front of her.

Was the howling a signal of pursuit, had it only been a warning, or was it for someone else?

There was no way of telling.

She only knew she had to continue moving, counting herself lucky that the road was all downhill. She prayed that Lee would pop out of the woods along the way to help her.

Time passed and darkness was complete. No streetlights, no cars. Just the sound of her breathing and her soles hard on the road.

She slowed reluctantly to a walk when a stitch worked its way across her right side. A glance back, and as far as she could tell there was no one behind her.

Trotting for a hundred yards.

Walking again.

Spinning around abrupdy, half hoping that she would see whoever it was, whatever it was, that she knew had to be back there.

Midway down, as the lights of Staines began to brighten the sky, she wondered with a suddenness that made her grunt if it wasn't all a trick. The others had escaped, and maybe the aliens were merely herding her, goading her along.

The thought stopped her.

And as she turned to look back up the road, she heard the faint growl of an automobile. Headlights touched the trees, swept away, returned, and she ran for the shoulder of the road, dropped down the slope behind it and hid in a tangle of ground ivy and shrubs.

If it was a car she didn't recognize, she decided to take the risk and try to flag it down. She would ask to be taken to the center of town, and from there she'd make her way back to Mrs. Chang.

She refused to consider the alternative.

And when the night became a sheet of glaring white, she narrowed her eyes, watching as the car moved at a near crawl past the place where she was crouching.

Oh, no, she thought, lowering her head in defeat.

It was a white Mercedes.

Monica Holt behind the wheel.

And someone else inside was aiming a flashlight—directly at her.

Ten

THE NARROW BEAM ARCHED OVER HER HEAD AS she pushed herself into the ground, her fingers grabbing at the ivy, anticipating being discovered.

But there was no cry of discovery, and the car moved on.

The flashlight stabbed elsewhere, erratically—at the brush, the trees, sweeping the area.

And just as quickly as the feeling that all was lost had come over her, it vanished in a resurgence of positive determination. And a few seconds later Jennifer risked raising her head to watch the white automobile's maddeningly slow progress down the hill. The brilliant taillights flared like the red eyes of an angry monster. The beam of the flashlight winked off for a moment, came on again, and resumed its slow search.

Cautiously, she pushed herself to her hands and knees, then into a crouch. Suddenly she was reminded of the harrowing night she and Marysue had plunged headlong down the steep, wooded slope just ahead of pursuing aliens, and how, only by chance, she had been found by Lee and taken to Conrad's house.

She couldn't do it again—go through the woods. Before, she had been propelled by blind panic; now, she wouldn't be able to move half as fast without injuring herself, perhaps seriously, and there was no time left to risk it.

Just as she knew then that she couldn't risk going to the Changs.

In order to remain free, she would have to double back to the campus and hope that either Marysue, Conrad, or Lee was still in the area and able to join her.

And if none of them was, then she'd have to go on to the den alone. What she would do there she didn't yet know, but at that moment she was struck by the realization that it was her only option left.

A shudder lifted her shoulders and tightened her chest. A deep breath to calm herself.

Time, she reminded herself, and she hurried onto the road, starting back up the hill. She wiped the perspiration from her face with a sleeve, jammed her hands deep into her pockets, and wished it wasn't so *cold*.

Less than a dozen steps later another glow of headlights bleached the dark from the trees. This time the car was coming from Staines, and she ducked swiftly back into the woods. Monica hadn't had time to get all the way down. Had she turned around? Maybe it was someone else.

Stifling her speculating, she crossed her fingers and waited, noting that the automobile was moving much faster than the Mercedes had, and she prayed that she'd have better luck.

Again the white glare, and again the growl of an engine, and again she dropped to the ground and stared hard at the black shape behind the lights, trying to will an outline to appear, trying to make an identification before the car was past.

And when it came abreast of her she knew it wasn't Holt. It was a different car, one she recognized vaguely, and she leaped instantly to her feet, waving her arms frantically and yelling, running onto the road and following the vehicle as it continued upward.

She screamed as loud as she could.

The taillights brightened as the car slowed. The passenger door opened and a familiar voice said, "Get in, Jenny, quickly!"

The car continued up the hill. Jennifer noted that its interior smelled of oil and cigar smoke, cracked leather and sweat. The backseat was crowded with something she couldn't see in the dark; her fingers touched wood and oily metal before drawing back. The green glow from the dashboard was weak, but sufficient for her to see Jack Rumbel hunched behind the wheel and Marlene Chang beside him.

"I don't understand," she gasped, out of breath from the shock of seeing the two adults together.

"There isn't much time," Mrs. Chang said kindly. "For now, let's just say that I've convinced Detective Rumbel here not to send you all to prison."

The policeman grunted; it may even have been a laugh.

"The important thing is," the woman continued, "that you're all right."

"I am. I think," she added and turned to look out the rear window. "That car—"

Mrs. Chang waited patiently, and finally Jennifer pulled herself together and gave a shortened version of what had happened since they'd left the house that morning. Rumbel slowed when she explained about Esther, Monica, and Barbara and sped up when she described the encounter with Dramon and the subsequent flight into the woods.

"Now I don't know where any of them are," she said, feeling the tears begin to sting her eyes. "Mrs. Chang, I'm so sorry, but we couldn't wait, and now—"

"It's all right, dear," the woman said. "Conrad's all right."

And she told Jennifer that she had just received a frantic call from her son telling her that he had managed to get himself trapped on campus with Marysue. The call was too short for her to get any details, but as soon as she had hung up, she contacted Rumbel to help her with Conrad's escape.

It was then that Jennifer looked at what was beside her on the seat, and she backed fearfully into the corner. There were at least two shotguns and a rifle, and on the floor behind the driver a small wooden crate with a rope handle.

When she looked up, she saw the detective staring at her in the rearview mirror.

"Kids," he grumbled, "are a pain you know where."

And, miraculously, he gave her a brief smile before directing his attention once again to the road. The main gate of the academy was visible now, and immediately he pulled over and switched off the lights, ran his hands nervously over the steering wheel and shook his head.

"Too many lights," he complained.

Mrs. Chang leaned closer to the windshield.

"Zucco said he'd try to get to the gate." She pointed to the entrance. "But I don't see him. Maybe he's hiding on the other side."

"No," Jennifer said and opened the back door. "That's not the gate he means."

Before either of them could stop her, she slipped out and disappeared into the trees along the wall.

A needled bough slapped her across the cheek, and she ducked away from the stinging pain, nearly turning her ankle on a half-buried rock. Nevertheless, she didn't slow down and she didn't try to move silently; there were too many leaves scattered on the ground, too many broken twigs, and she had to move fast. The car couldn't stay long on the side of the road. At any moment the Mercedes might come roaring back.

She reached the gate in the woods.

It was open.

A gust of wind drove her hair into her eyes, snapping cold at her cheeks and hands.

She listened, trying to separate the sound of the night into the component parts, searching for a warning that a trap had been laid, or Dramon had left someone behind in case she returned.

Finally she could stand it no longer. "Zucco," she whispered. "Beauford!"

No answer.

With a hand on either side of the entrance, she leaned in, looking quickly side to side.

"Conrad, it's Jenny!"

No answer.

Oh, no, she thought.

"Marysue! It's me!"

And nearly screamed when a quaking voice said behind her, "Prove it."

She whirled around, stumbled, and fell heavily against the wall, one arm up to protect herself when she saw a dark figure holding a twisted branch over its head.

"Marysue, it's me," she said.

The figure stepped forward, and Marysue gasped as she threw her arms around her. They embraced for a long moment before separating, and Jennifer told her about the waiting car as she grabbed the girl's hand and started to drag her to the road. Then she stopped.

"Wait a minute. Where's Zucco?"

"Here," he answered and dropped lightly from a branch over her head. "Richmond wouldn't climb the tree, so she had to do the checking."

But he wasn't smiling, and Jennifer led them quickly to the car. Marysue joined her in back while Conrad squeezed in front with his mother. The reunion between mother and son was accomplished by a quick but strong hug. Then Rumbel started the engine and drove slowly past the academy's entrance.

As he did, Conrad told them that they'd gotten the things Jennifer had wanted from the lab, but they'd been spotted by O'Malley. "She had a bandage around her head," he said. "What happened?"

"An allergy to glass," Jennifer remarked dryly.

Conrad exchanged puzzled glances with his mother before telling them that he and Marysue had managed to hide in the Student Union and used the public telephone there to call home. "Then we came out here and waited." He rubbed his arms briskly. "Boy, it was cold in that tree."

"Where's Lee?" Marysue asked.

"I don't know," Jennifer said. "The last time I saw him—"

She stopped and swallowed, not wanting to believe that he might have been captured.

They drove on in silence, slowly, until Conrad happened to look over the back of the seat and his mouth dropped open. "That's an arsenal," he said.

"I already met one of them things," Rumbel growled. "I ain't taking any chances." He shifted uncomfortably. "You know how to use one, boy?"

"Yes."

Mrs. Chang said nothing, but Jennifer saw her stiffen.

"Good. How about the girls?"

"Are you kidding?" Marysue said.

"No," Jennifer answered.

Mrs. Chang said quietly, "I'll take the rifle."

Conrad only stared at her. No one else said a word, not until they reached the narrow trail leading to the Witch's Eye. Then Rumbel pulled over and doused the lights without cutting the engine. With a grunt he turned awkwardly until he was facing them, and Jennifer saw his face clearly for the first time—it was bruised where he'd been struck the night of the fight.

"Tell me about the lab," he said.

Conrad looked at Jennifer, who nodded. Then he reached into the inner pocket of his coat and pulled out something wrapped in cloth. Slowly he peeled the cloth away and held out his hand.

Mrs. Chang said, "If that's what I think it is, you're lucky you didn't blow yourself up."

Rumbel leaned forward to see what Conrad held and shook his head. "Don't get it."

"It was Jennifer's idea," the boy said. "These four test tubes have a small lump of sodium at the bottom, and that's oil it's floating in." He glanced at the detective and pointed. "The others are filled only with water. Strap them together like they are now, throw them like grenades, and when the glass breaks and the sodium hits the air and mixes with the water, you've got a fire that won't quit."

Rumbel looked at him skeptically, and Conrad grinned. "Trust me," he said. "It'll work." Then he looked back at Jennifer. "We were going to head for the den, that was the plan I made with Lee. He was supposed to come with you." He shrugged. "Then it all fell apart."

Jennifer felt a sudden dryness in her throat. "Lee," she said quietly.

"Right," Conrad said. "With any kind of luck, he's already there."

Eleven

"ALL RIGHT," RUMBEL SAID TERSELY. "IT'S TIME."

Things moved too quickly after that for Jennifer. She felt she had fallen into a nightmare.

The car swung onto the trail, its rear tires kicking up stones that cracked like hail against the frame. Rumbel paid scant attention to the branches scraping along the sides and roof, seemingly content merely to grip the steering wheel and not stop until they broke into the irregular clearing in front of the small lake known as Witch's Eye. Then he braked and switched off the lights at the same time; he was out of the car before the engine stopped ticking over.

Jennifer climbed out and looked at the small dark lake, the two deserted cabins on either side of the clearing, and couldn't help thinking of it as a graveyard made especially for them.

An owl screeched.

"Y'know," the rumpled detective said as they walked up to join him, "I thought about telling the chief all about this. I thought about it hard."

"Why didn't you?" Jennifer asked.

He snorted. "Are you kidding, girl? What do you think he'd say if I told him I'd been beaten up by someone dressed in a wolf suit?"

Jennifer didn't answer; she knew the problem all too well.

"Why did you come to help us now?" Marysue asked.

"Marlene."

"Mom?" Conrad said, astonished.

Mrs. Chang smiled. "Jack and I go back a long way, Zucco. Long before I ever met your father. We grew up next door to each other. And we hated each other's guts." She laughed and put a hand on the man's arm, and Jennifer couldn't help but smile at his embarrassment. "But I never thought he was stupid. So after you told me your story, I went to him and gave him a chance to tell me you were—I don't know."

"Lying," Conrad said softly, disappointment in his tone.

"No, dear," she said, going over to lay her hands on his shoulders. "But you have to admit, confirmation was needed. Isn't that what you're always telling me—never take anything at face value until you've made all the tests? Well, what better test than Jack here?"

Conrad looked into his mother's eyes, and it was a long time before he nodded.

And the moment he did, Rumbel said, "Enough of that," grabbed the weapons from the back of the car, handed them out, and took ammunition from the wooden crate. Without a word he loaded the shotguns and the rifle, then gave them extra shells to stuff into their pockets.

Conrad handed the test-tube grenades to Jennifer and Marysue.

"Lee," Jennifer said out loud, "what if he's not there? What if—"

"I don't know," Conrad said. "But we're here now, and we can't go back."

They stood for a moment longer, listening, waiting for someone to give the word.

At last, unable to stand it any longer, Jennifer took the first step, and her excitement overrode her fear of the danger she knew she was walking into.

After all this time, she thought as she headed for the path on the righthand side of the clearing. After all this time, we're finally going to do it.

The lake shimmered in the moonlight, the ripples like ribbons of silver spreading in the wind. But the forest was black, the path almost impossible to see once they moved into the woods, and Rumble fished a flashlight from his pocket and passed it forward to Conrad, who had taken the lead. Marysue was directly behind him, then Mrs. Chang and Jennifer. Rumbel brought up the rear, spending as much time looking back as he did to the front.

Ballad Hill rose as a black wall beside them.

There were no sounds of nightbirds, nothing scurried in the brush.

At the next, smaller clearing Conrad had them pause for a brief rest before moving on. When they continued, they moved more slowly and closer together doing their best to keep their presence unknown to the aliens.

Jennifer began to worry.

It all came down to this, and if something should go wrong, they wouldn't have a second chance. Arrogance or not, the aliens wouldn't let them escape.

And they wouldn't let them live.

Rumbel puffed heavily behind her, and fifteen minutes after they had entered the woods again, he touched her back with a finger.

"How'd you get into this?" he asked in a husky whisper.

She thought back to the summer session she had attended before the regular semester began.

She thought of the friends she had made, and the friends who had betrayed her. She thought of the home-sickness and the hard work, the bland food in the dining hall and the impromptu parties in the dorm.

She thought of slanting green eyes.

She thought of the howl of a wolf.

"I don't know," she answered truthfully. "I got curious one day, that's all."

A handful of seconds passed before he said, "Curiosity killed the cat, y'know, kid." He paused. "But cats have nine lives."

Startled, she looked over her shoulder, but his face was hidden by shifting moon shadows. And then, before she could stop herself, she asked, "Why do you hate kids so much?"

He had no time to answer.

Suddenly Conrad hissed at them, snapped off the flash-light, and dropped to one knee. The others did the same, and the only sound was the soft clank of weapons shifting in their grips.

Jennifer patted her righthand pocket, assuring herself that the two makeshift fire bombs were still there.

The darkness was complete in spite of the moon.

The trees and overhead branches formed a tunnel that pressed down on them and chilled them.

And Jennifer listened, hearing nothing but Rumbel's labored breathing until, suddenly, there was a rustling in the underbrush to her left.

Someone was moving through the woods, but she was unable to determine whether he was heading up the slope toward them or away from them toward the lake. But whoever it was seemed not to be concerned about being overheard, and Jennifer was puzzled. Surely one of the aliens—Dramon, Holt, or O'Malley—had gotten a message to the den; surely the alien pack must realize it was in danger.

Unless, she thought as the movement faded, it was a trap.

She blinked rapidly as the idea blossomed—a trap. The wolf-creatures knew they were coming, and they were waiting. Just waiting for the humans to show themselves.

A minute passed, and five more, before Conrad signaled them to continue moving.

Jennifer couldn't shake the feeling that they were making a mistake, and she wished Lee were there to give her some guidance. She pressed her way forward, past Mrs. Chang and Marysue, to tap Conrad's shoulder and tell him what she feared. He didn't stop. He continued on, but his brusque nod told her he had already thought the same thing. He turned and quietly assured her that he wasn't going to lead them into an ambush.

She wondered.

And she couldn't help but think that their chances would have been better if Lee had been there. The idea that his leg was seriously injured frightened her; the idea that the injury would stop him from coming to help them frightened her even more.

Now there were only five of them, no matter how heavily armed, and the aliens probably numbered two or three times that—with weapons of their own.

Ten minutes later they reached the small clearing that stood just above the entrance to the den. Most of the grass and foliage was dead and gray, the moonlight now bright enough to highlight the destruction.

The wind keened.

There was no other sound.

Conrad ordered them down again, but it was too late.

In the center stood Esther Fine, wearing a peacoat and jeans. And though her face was still human, her hands were thickly covered in fur—one holding a gun while the other snugly gripped the back of Pauline Klopher's neck.

The librarian was a short woman, wearing a heavy dark sweater and dark slacks. Her long, gray-streaked black hair was hanging over her shoulders, and her large eyes widened in astonishment when Conrad stepped boldly into the clearing, the shotgun in his hands.

"Well, Zucco," Esther said, her voice cool. "You can put it down now and bring your friends out into the open where I can see them."

"Are you all right, Mrs. Klopher?" Conrad asked anxiously.

"Well as I can be," she answered in a hoarse voice and winced when Esther Fine tightened her grip and pushed the barrel of the gun against her temple. "I'm going to have a headache when this is over though."

"C'mon!" the alien ordered angrily. "We haven't got all night."

Conrad glared at her, then sighed and carefully placed the gun at his feet. A look over his shoulder brought his mother and Marysue into the clearing with him. Jennifer followed a moment later.

"Where's fat boy?" Esther demanded, staring past them to the trail.

"Waiting at the car," Jennifer answered quickly. "He's supposed to make sure none of you gets out."

Fine laughed and shook her head. "When are you going to learn? Stupid. Really stupid." She looked at each of them in disgust, then ordered Conrad to pick up the shotgun and rifle and cradle them in his arms, keeping his hands away from them and pointing upward. When he had done as she commanded, she jerked her head toward the path. "You wanted in, Field? So go in."

Jennifer started forward, stopped abruptly, and turned to face her. "No," she said, displaying more calm than she felt. "No, I don't think so."

Fine obviously couldn't believe it. She shook Mrs. Klopher and the gun, the message clear, and widened her eyes in amazement when Jennifer only took a pair of short steps to her left, forcing the alien to turn slightly in order to keep an eye on her.

"You're asking for trouble, Field," the alien warned. "I don't have any orders to keep Klopher alive."

Jennifer shrugged and forced herself to continue staring ahead even when she heard Marysue gasp. "You're going to kill us anyway," she said. "Why not here?"

Esther looked perplexed.

"A good point, young lady," Mrs. Klopher said. "No sense dying underground when we have all this fresh air, right?"

Mrs. Chang, her hands out to show that they were empty, moved to stand between her son and Marysue, the three of them on the alien's left. Jennifer saw her grip their arms and force them back a step. And another.

"Hold it!" Fine ordered, aiming the gun at them. "Right there. Not another step."

"Why not?" said Jack Rumbel, stepping out of the shadows.

Esther turned sharply, swinging the gun around, and gave Mrs. Klopher the chance to twist away and lash out, kicking Esther on the shin.

The gun fired harmlessly into the ground at the top of the clearing, and Rumbel fired. Once. Catching the alien in the center of its chest and slamming it to its back.

Jennifer gaped in horror, deafened by the retort and not hearing the sudden spate of orders until Mrs. Chang grabbed her arm, and she realized the others had already retrieved their weapons and were racing for the downward trail.

All hope of concealment was gone.

Like it or not, the attack had begun.

Twelve

SEVERAL YARDS DOWN THE NARROW PATH THE way was blocked by a large, flat-topped boulder from the top of which they had seen the entrance to the den. Now they moved past it, not waiting, knowing that the gunshot must have been heard by the aliens. Knowing that they had to get below ground. There had to be things down there—equipment, experiments, life support systems—that couldn't stand to be damaged.

It wasn't going to be easy.

But neither were they going to make it easy for the aliens.

They ran then, and Jennifer bade her parents a silent goodbye as she plunged through the brush and into a space too small to be called a clearing. It was there that she had seen the camouflaged opening.

But it was open now. The entrance open and waiting for them.

A trap, she thought again: It's a trap.

Until a disheveled Lee popped out from behind a tree and spread his arms to indicate the hole in the ground. "Nice work, huh? There ain't a lock in the universe I can't pick."

The others were too stunned to move, but Jennifer flung herself into his arms, hugging him and kissing him soundly.

"Where have you been?" she demanded in a loud whisper. "We were almost killed back there."

"Nah," he said. "You're too tough." But his flippant words were canceled by the deep concern in his eyes.

Rumbel grumbled under his breath, pushed them aside, and peered into the hole. "We gonna wait for them or what?" he said.

"Later," Jennifer told Lee as he stared in disbelief at the detective. She was the first to follow the policeman into the hole, knowing that if she waited, if she let someone else go first, all her nerve would flee.

At first it was dark, so dark she felt the fear she'd been keeping at bay rush into her throat. And the rungs of the metal ladder were bitterly cold in her hands. But by the time she reached the bottom, less than two dozen feet from the surface, the tunnel had brightened, and she stood to one side, amazed at what she saw.

The tunnel led in only one direction—gently downward and to the left—its sides and high roof braced by heavy woodlike beams, the dirt floor packed so hard that there was no sign of anyone having passed through. The hole looked as if it had been cleanly bored by some huge machine, and the polished support beams gave off a subtle glow that made a flashlight unnecessary.

The tunnel was at once strange but familiar, not unfriendly. But it was the silence that made her rub her arms for warmth. A deep, almost audible silence that remained undisturbed, echoless, even as the others followed behind.

She wondered if it was the silence that stretched between the stars.

She wondered if it was the silence in which the aliens lived on their home planet.

Her eyes closed briefly. Field, she told herself, this is no time to get spooked.

When they were all down, the detective and Conrad held a hurried conference, then took the rifle from Mrs. Chang and gave it to Lee. She didn't object, and Lee didn't protest when he was placed at the back of the group. There was no time for argument, and when he moved, Jennifer just in front of him, it was clear that he was still favoring his leg.

They were almost running by the time the ladder faded from sight, but still none of the creatures had attempted to intercept them. Jennifer couldn't understand it: the sound of the gun should have brought the entire alien colony on the run. She told herself to be thankful for small favors, and she concentrated on not tripping over her own feet and looking from side to side to check for other tunnels leading off the main one.

"Ahead, just a little farther, I think." Pauline Klopher was scanning the walls for signs that only she could read. "I got a pretty fair tour of the place while I was here—just past this next beam. Here it is!"

The door set in the side of the tunnel was steel, solid enough to explain why none of the aliens had come running at the sound of the shot; no noise could get through the layers of steel. And the single window set at the top of the door was obviously designed to keep one atmosphere out and the other in. The window was a bit too high for the diminutive librarian, but she didn't need to look in. As the others peered through, she told them what they were seeing.

"It's one of their laboratories. There are at least four labs and some living spaces—and at least a dozen wolves. I was only in this one once, but I'm pretty sure they keep a normal atmosphere inside—earth normal, that is."

Jennifer took her turn at the window. "What are those things on the tables?"

"Costumes, I guess you could call them."

Costumes. Flesh-colored costumes.

Costumes to make the aliens look human.

Jennifer craned around to see as much of the lab as she could. "There's no one in there." She stepped back from the door, grabbed the handle, and pulled. Nothing happened.

"Try pushing," Mrs. Chang suggested.

Jennifer pushed. Still nothing. But the handle twisted when she tried it, and then the door pushed in easily, almost too easily, and Jennifer was inside.

The rest slipped in behind her and let the door close. It was a long room, just wide enough for a single, comfortable aisle between the rows of tables next to the walls, narrow enough that there was nothing more than they had seen from the door. On each of the tables was a mound, five feet long or more, of pinkish, rubbery material, the same material that Jennifer had ripped from Monica Holt's face.

After the first touch, none of the invading humans could bear to do more than poke at the synthetic flesh, except Conrad. His scientific imagination was seized by the marvel of the stuff, by how well it imitated the color and texture of human skin and muscle, how the surface of it bore the tiny hairs and pores and slight imperfections of humans. He stretched it, testing its strength and flexibility, and stuck his hand inside the mask to examine the features. For a moment he squinted at it, trying to decide why it looked so familiar. "Lee!"

Fawkes turned to him raising the rifle automatically. "Yeah?"

"Come look at this."

The others came, too, but Conrad held the mask so that only Lee could see it clearly.

"Look familiar?"

Lee looked closely, but shook his head. "I don't see what you're getting at."

"Put reddish brown hair on it," Conrad prompted.

Again Lee concentrated on the face, draping it with auburn hair. "Oh, no." He looked from the mask to Jennifer, staring at her wide-eyed, then back at the mask.

"Exactly," Conrad said.

"Now we know why they never killed us. They were waiting for these to be ready."

Jennifer pushed Lee aside and grabbed the mask. She had to force herself to ignore the feel of it and concentrate on looking. The imitation skin, intended for the use of one of the aliens, wasn't quite finished, and hadn't had its hair attached yet, but the face was unmistakable and familiar. Very familiar.

It was her face.

None of the other costumes were as close to being finished or modeled after people they recognized, but there was one about Marysue's size, and another large one that might have been intended to become Conrad. He ripped that one grimly, splitting it down the middle and shredding it into tiny pieces until Lee interrupted.

"Nothing here in my size. I feel left out. Where do I go to complain?"

Conrad just stared at him for a second, then stifled the giggle that broke across his face. Marysue couldn't stifle hers; Mrs. Chang joined in, and Lee, and then they were all laughing, falling back against the tables, throwing bits of synthetic flesh at one another.

Their collective giggling fit passed as quickly as it had hit, but had served one purpose. It left the raiding party more relaxed. They remained in the lab just long enough to destroy as many of the costumes and as much of the equipment as they could. Then they continued farther down the long, curving corridor.

They passed a couple more doors that Mrs. Klopher identified as storage closets and another lab where she had been poked and prodded by the aliens' researchers. It was empty then.

They went deeper.

Mrs. Klopher stumbled once, more from fatigue than anything else, and Conrad immediately left Maiysue's side to put his arm around the older woman. She nodded her head in thanks, but insisted she would either make it on her own or she wouldn't make it at all.

Zucco smiled, but he didn't release her.

Rumbel lifted an arm to stop them, and they all moved close to him.

"Who feels lucky?" he muttered.

The tunnel forked some thirty yards ahead, and there was no indication of which way they should go.

"Do you know anything about these different tunnels?" Jennifer asked Mrs. Klopher.

"I know positively that there are living quarters to the right, and I think there's a laboratory. Maybe some other chambers as well. To the left there is a laboratory, and I don't know what else. I haven't been there."

"We'll have to split up," Mrs. Chang said reluctantly. "We have to investigate both."

Rumbel divided the group in half—Conrad, Marysue, and Mrs. Klopher were to go with him to the right, the others were to take the left fork. Fifteen minutes, he said, and then they were to turn around and return. No longer. No farther.

He made sure Lee had enough ammunition for the rifle, then surprisingly shook the boy's hand before waving his group on.

Lee stared after him until Jennifer tugged at his arm. Then he took a deep breath, smiled humorlessly, and followed Jennifer and Mrs. Chang without as much as a sideways glance.

Thirteen

FIVE MINUTES INTO THEIR EXCURSION, THE ONLY difference Jennifer noted was that the tunnel had leveled off. She had no idea in what direction they were heading, but she suspected they were now deep under the next hill behind Ballad.

And still the extraordinary silence.

And still the feeling that they weren't alone.

She kept looking over her shoulder, unnerved when she didn't see anything, unnerved even more when she realized that their moving through the beams' glow produced no shadows. It was as if they were running through a dream, and twice Jennifer had to slap lightly at her face to prevent herself from falling into a hypnotic stupor.

Then Lee stopped abruptly.

The tunnel curved sharply to the right, and though they could see nothing beyond, Jennifer soon heard the unmistakable low and muffled sounds of machinery at work. Blindly she reached for Lee's hand and squeezed it, then looked at Mrs. Chang, who was holding one of the fire bombs in her left hand and rubbing it thoughtfully with her thumb.

Lee motioned them to stay where they were, and he moved forward, remaining close to the wall. He held the muzzle of the rifle up though his finger remained on the

105

trigger. When he vanished around the curve, Jennifer closed her eyes briefly. And when she opened them, she saw Mrs. Chang watching her with a small knowing smile.

Mrs. Chang winked, tilted her head, and began to follow Lee.

Jennifer didn't protest. She remained in the woman's wake, her hand sliding into her pocket to feel her test tubes. She uttered a soft, hissing sigh of relief when her fingers closed around them.

She clamped her lips shut when they reached the spot where the curve abruptly ended and she saw Lee standing still and staring at the tunnel's end. When he heard them, he spun around, rifle at the ready, and scowled when Mrs. Chang and Jennifer hurried up beside him. Jennifer stood behind him, not believing her eyes.

The tunnel ended just ahead, at a large, gleaming metal door which appeared to be as thick and heavy as the door to a bank vault. In the center was a circular window. The hum of machinery came from behind it.

Jennifer and Lee looked at each other, then inched forward until they were standing on either side of the window. Jennifer, despite the cool, underground air, began to sweat, and she wiped her palms on her legs before taking a deep breath and looking in.

She almost gasped aloud.

On the other side of the door was a cavern fully one hundred feet across and at least that high. It was filled with laboratory equipment she could put no name to though it seemed tantalizingly familiar. But along the smoothly carved walls were a number of items she recognized immediately—cone-shaped capsules with single ports in their centers, single doors on each one.

They were atmosphere chambers, where the aliens could breathe their own air without using the special patches they were forced to wear on their sides when they moved about above ground.

She was about to let the others have a look at what she'd found when she saw them—a dozen or more aliens moving slowly about the tables, checking on glass cages of small forest animals, examining glass cases with plants inside. Two of them were in Ionian form—one whom Jennifer didn't recognize, but the other, bandaged head and all, was ummistakably Barbara O'Malley. The others were all in their natural, wolflike state.

None of them were wearing special breathing apparatus, and as Jennifer stepped aside to let Lee have a look, she knew suddenly that the door was thick because it was holding in the atmosphere the aliens were trying to re-create above ground. The door had no handle like the one on the other lab.

Lee took her arm and pulled her back around the curve, Mrs. Chang following.

"I didn't see a latch or knob or anything," he whispered helplessly. "Are we going to have to wait for one of them to come out?"

Jennifer looked at her watch. "Our time's almost up. Maybe we should go back and get the others."

They both looked at Conrad's mother, who for the first time didn't know what to do. When she shrugged, the gesture told them she was feeling as torn as they—to leave, now, when the aliens were still unaware of them, seemed foolish; yet there was nothing they could do. Not until they learned what, if anything, the others had discovered.

"All right," Lee said firmly. "Mrs. Chang, you go get Rumbel and the others. Jenny and I will wait here. If anything happens, we'll run, make a lot of noise, and meet you back at the ladder."

Jennifer wasn't sure that was wise, or even made sense, but Mrs. Chang wasted no time. She nodded, hugged them both as she handed Jennifer her bomb, and ran off. And as soon as she was gone, Lee made sure there was a shell in the rifle's chamber.

The crack of the bolt slamming home startled Jennifer. Her stomach lurched, her throat became dry, and she could hear her blood pounding in her ears. Then, as Lee watched, she stepped into view of the door and stared at it.

"They've done it, you know," she told him softly. "Lee, they've done it. They've changed the atmosphere in there."

And as the horror of what she said swept over them, her legs trembled, her hands refused to work, and she had to lean against the wall for a moment, to wait for her composure to return.

And when it did, anger came with it. A cold, reasoning rage that hardened her eyes and forced Lee to look away.

"Can you shoot that thing?" she asked, nodding at the rifle.

"Best shot in the West," he answered with a weak smile.

She grabbed his shoulder and pulled him around the comer. "Can you shoot out that window? Fast?"

"Jen, that stuff's thick!"

"Is it bullet-proof?"

"I—I don't know, how could I?"

She looked at him and held up one of her tiny bombs.

"Whoa," he said. "Do you know what'll happen even if the glass breaks? All that stuff they breathe in there is going to come out here. We'll—"

"But it's not under pressure," she interrupted, trying to put all the urgency she felt into every word. "The atmospheric pressure is the same in there as it is out here, or close enough not to make a difference. If you can get through that glass fast enough, and I can get these bombs in there..."

They stared at each other for several long seconds, each knowing that that step would be the last, that after it, if they failed, all else would fail as well.

"What about the others?"

A check of her watch. "We'll give Mrs. Chang ten minutes, okay? Ten minutes. By that time..." And she shrugged.

Jennifer held Lee's hand tightly as though trying to say everything without speaking a word; Lee stared at the opposite wall, his expression completely blank.

Finally she roused herself, checked the time, and nodded.

And closed her eyes briefly.

Then Lee said with a one-sided smile, "Well, it sure hasn't been dull knowing you, Field, you know that?"

She grinned. "You're not so bad yourself, Fawkes."

And before either of them could think again, he turned, put the rifle to his shoulder, and pulled the trigger.

The report was nearly deafening in the enclosed space, but she ordered herself not to flinch, not to run. Instead she concentrated on the bombs she held in each hand.

The window webbed at the first impact, worse at the second and third, and suddenly sprouted a small hole at the fourth. Inside, she could see blurred activity, dark figures running, the sound of breaking glass.

Lee fired again, and again, then ran with her to the door and used the butt of the rifle to punch at the glass.

An alien appeared on the other side and howled in rage.

Others crowded in behind him, and Lee spun the weapon in his hands and fired into the crowd. A scream. A flare of blood.

And in that one brief moment when the door was clear, Jennifer shoved him aside and threw in the bombs.

And ran.

As fast as she could, she ran with Lee beside her, puzzled when she stumbled, frightened when she felt herself gasping for air. She realized then as they swung into the tunnel's endless curve that standing before the door as they had, had exposed them to the very atmosphere they had been trying to defeat.

She grabbed Lee's arm to keep from falling.

Lee lurched against her drunkenly and knocked them both into the wall.

The rifle fell to the ground, and he left it.

Running.

Hearing only the thunder of their own footsteps until that thunder was replaced by a great rush of wind and a cloud of dust that knocked them off their feet, just as the sound of explosions reached them.

Like a cannonade in a furious battle, the explosions echoed and bellowed through the tunnel, louder and louder until Jennifer thought she would scream.

She scrambled to her feet, dragged Lee to his, and they ran again, the temperature rising slowly, steadily, drenching them with perspiration, thickening the air to make it even more difficult to breathe.

Running.

The explosions more distant but no less vicious.

The pulsing waves of heat washing over them, causing them to stumble, to stagger, adding weight to their shoulders and lead to their feet.

Debris began to fall from the roof—great clouds of dust, clods of dirt, and showers of rock rained on them. Jennifer folded her arms over her head for protection and cried out when she couldn't see Lee anymore. He answered from somewhere just ahead, and she forced herself on until she tripped over his prone figure.

"My leg," he gasped, grime and sweat coating his face.

She hooked a hand under his shoulder and pulled him to his feet, wrapped an arm around his waist and started to half walk, half drag him until, only a few steps later, he stopped and shook his head.

"Can't," he gasped. "Jen, go ahead. I'll be all right."

She looked back, squinting into the windstorm. The explosions were less powerful and less frequent, but as the ground began to shake beneath them and more debris spilled from the walls and the roof, she knew what she had to do.

She dragged him on.

He helped as best he could, but by the time the tunnel began to slope up again and she knew they were nearing the fork, each step he took was accompanied by a grunt of pain.

"C'mon, Lee," she said angrily. "C'mon, come *on!*"

Step — "come" — step — *"on"* — step — "come"— step — *"on"*

Over and over again.

Numbing her mind to everything but moving. Reminding herself that each step was one step closer to the ladder, one step farther away from the holocaust that raged behind them.

Over and over again.

Through the dust, the falling rock. Falling once when the ground heaved. Screaming her frustration and constantly pulling Lee up and out.

Crying. Shrieking. Urging him, pleading with him, ordering him not to quit, not when they were so close, not when they were almost home.

Choking on the dust, spitting the dirt out, ignoring the pain that flamed across her back and across the back of her head.

Falling.

Rising.

Not missing a step when, without warning, the tunnel fell dark.

A darkness so complete she saw dancing lights in front of her eyes; a darkness so total she was sure she heard footsteps running up behind her. The explosions in the vast laboratory hadn't ended, and neither had the quaking, or the slow collapse of the tunnel; yet she soon became convinced that someone was following them, and she didn't dare call out now because it might not be Marysue or any of the others—it might be one of *them*, an alien survivor.

And suddenly she slammed into a wall, and they both fell heavily to the ground.

Up, she told herself. Get up, Jenny, get up, get up!

With her hands out she stood, swayed, and sobbed when her fingers brushed over the rungs of the ladder. Quickly she grabbed Lee, told him what she had found, and urged him to climb. Pushing him, shoving him, then following and falling over him when she, too, reached the fresh air and rolled onto her back to gulp, to grin, to sob, and finally to crawl to her hands and knees and look around.

There was blessed moonlight still, and great billows of dust flew into the air. The ground still shook, and as she watched she saw what must have been a section of tunnel collapse with a loud rumbling, taking several trees with it.

"Lee, let's go," she said and urged him to his feet again, up the slope until, at last, exhaustion made her fall just before the boulder.

"Conrad?" he whispered, his voice laden with pain.

"I don't know," she said. "I don't—I don't know."

And froze when she heard something scrape across the top of the boulder.

Slowly she moved a few feet down the slope, staggered to her feet, and looked up.

There in the moonlight stood a dark figure, its face in shadow, though she could see the fur on its body.

Fourteen

"YOU DID IT, FIELD," SAID MONICA HOLT.

The ground trembled, another section of tunnel collapsed.

Jennifer stepped back fearfully, not wanting to believe her friends might have died for nothing.

"You did it," Holt said again. "But you're not going to live to enjoy it."

"Monica, please," Jennifer said.

The alien laughed, long and loud, ending with its head thrown back, its fangs bared, howling rage and despair, before looking down again.

And slowly lowered itself into a crouch, snarling, slanted green eyes glowing.

Jennifer looked frantically for something she could use as a weapon, then raised her weary hands in loose fists and waited. There was nothing else she could do. She was too tired to run, and she wasn't going to die without a fight.

The alien tensed.

Lee moaned.

And Jennifer braced herself when the wolf-creature sprang into the air, threw herself to one side, and scrambled to her feet when it landed lightly, spun around, and laughed.

"I'm going to kill you," Holt said. "Just like you killed all mine."

And Jennifer was too weak to dodge again when the alien rose to leap; she waited, fists ready, thinking she might be able to get hold of its throat. Maybe Lee... maybe...

Suddenly there was a shot, and a howling scream, and the alien pitched forward onto its face, shook once, and was still.

And Jack Rumbel said, "Kid, you all right?"

They huddled by Witch's Eye, watching the water darken as the moon dropped below the hills. The night was cold, but they didn't feel it. The woods were filled with the sounds of the passing wind, but they didn't hear them.

Jennifer had no idea how long it had taken them to return to the clearing, but she knew they weren't quite ready to get back into the car and leave. Not yet. Not just yet.

Lee sat beside her, his arm around her shoulders, Conrad and Marysue on the other side. The adults were at Rumbel's automobile, talking quietly among themselves.

"When I write my memoirs," Marysue finally said in an exaggerated Virginia accent, "I am going to be sure I do not include this. Crawling around in the woods does not fit my image."

Mrs. Chang had reached the others, who had found only a dead end. It was their race to get out of the tunnel when the destruction began that Jennifer had heard. And in her haste to get Lee out of the way, she hadn't heard them take the ladder to safety.

"Actually," said Conrad, "all in all, I think we did pretty well." He looked over then. "Thanks to Jenny."

"You said it," Lee agreed, hugging her tightly. "She saved my life."

"All our lives," Conrad amended. "The whole world's life. The whole solar system. The—"

"Stick it, Zucco," Marysue told him. "You're going to embarrass the poor child."

Jennifer laughed with the others, but couldn't help a feeling of great sadness. So many had died, so many creatures from a planet she had never even read about—the knowledge that was lost, the opportunities. The waste of it all made her wonder. She knew that it had to have been done, but she also knew it would be a long time before she was truly convinced that what had been done was the only solution.

Still, she thought, being alive had a lot going for it.

"It's too bad about Mr. Overbrook," Marysue said, tossing a pebble into the water. "He was a nice guy."

"Yeah," Lee said. "Not bad for a grown-up."

"Well, they're not so bad, either," Conrad said, jerking a thumb over his shoulder.

"Tell me that when Rumbel marries your mother," Lee retorted with a grin, and Jennifer yelped when Conrad made a mock lunge across her to get at his throat.

Then, slowly they struggled to their feet and made their way to the car. Mrs. Chang insisted they all return to the house where their injuries could be treated and a meal prepared. No one objected. And no one mentioned telling their story to the authorities.

There was no sense in it. The laboratory was destroyed, the aliens defeated. All that was left now was getting on with their lives.

"My dears," Marysue said as she climbed into the back-seat, "I will never, but never, complain about exams or homework again."

"I wouldn't go that far," Conrad said, climbing in beside her. "But all that stuff's sure gonna seem tame."

Lee and Jennifer crowded in after them and looked at the others in the front seat. Rumbel was solemn, Mrs. Chang was grinning nervously, and in the middle, Pauline Klopher was taking several deep breaths.

Jennifer frowned and leaned forward. "Mrs. Klopher, are you all right?"

"Yes, dear, I think so."

The engine coughed to life, the headlights flared on, and the car lurched forward, toward the highway, toward home.

And as they sped past Thaler, Jennifer looked through the gates. Then turned and saw the others looking, too.

No one spoke, and no one objected when Mrs. Klopher asked the detective if he would mind stopping and backing up for a minute. He did as he was asked, but scowled when she directed him to drive through the gates and turn around.

But he did.

And Jennifer saw where she was looking and shook her head in denial.

"It can't be," Marysue said, speaking all their thoughts out loud.

But there was no wishing it away—there was a light in one of the three faculty houses on the far right side of the crescent.

And Jennifer knew that there was still one of them left, still one of them alive.

The light glowed in Peter Dramon's house.

And as Rumbel pulled back onto the highway, they heard a mournful howling as the moon vanished behind a cloud.

"Just a dog," Lee said quickly. "That's all. It's just a dog, right?"

"Sure," Jennifer said. And she knew she was lying.

Fast-paced, action-packed stories—the ultimate adventure/mystery series!

COMING SOON...
HAVE YOU SEEN
THE HARDY BOYS LATELY?

Beginning in April 1987, all-new Hardy Boys mysteries will be available in pocket-sized editions called THE HARDY BOYS CASEFILES.

Frank and Joe Hardy are eighties guys with eighties interests, living in Bayport, U.S.A. Their extracurricular activities include girlfriends, fast-food joints, hanging out at the mall and quad theaters. But computer whiz Frank and the charming, athletic Joe are deep into international intrigue and high-tech drama. The pace of these mysteries just never lets up!

For a sample of the *new* Hardy Boys, turn the page and enjoy an excerpt from DEAD ON TARGET and EVIL, INC., the first two books in THE HARDY BOYS CASE-FILES.

And don't forget to look for more of the new Hardy Boys and details about a great Hardy Boys contest in April!

THE HARDY BOYS CASEFILES™

Case #1
Dead on Target

A terrorist bombing sends Frank and Joe on a mission of revenge.

"GET OUT OF *my way, Frank!*" Joe Hardy shoved past his brother, shouting to be heard over the roar of the flames. Straight ahead, a huge fireball rose like a mushroom cloud over the parking lot. Flames shot fifty feet into the air, dropping chunks of wreckage—wreckage that just a moment earlier had been their yellow sedan. "Iola's in there! We've got to get her out!"

Frank stared, his lean face frozen in shock, as his younger brother ran straight for the billowing flames. Then he raced after Joe, catching him in a flying tackle twenty feet away from the blaze. Even at that distance they could feel the heat.

"Do you want to get yourself killed?" Frank yelled, rising to his knees.

Joe remained silent, his blue eyes staring at the wall of flame, his blond hair mussed by the fall.

Frank hauled his brother around, making Joe face him. "She wouldn't have lasted a second," he said, trying to soften the blow. "Face it, Joe."

For an instant, Frank thought the message had gotten through. Joe sagged against the concrete. Then he surged up again, eyes wild. "No! I can save her! Let go!"

Before Joe could get to his feet, Frank tackled him again, sending both of them tumbling along the ground. Joe began struggling, thrashing against his brother's grip. With near-maniacal strength, he broke Frank's hold, then started throwing wild punches at his brother, almost as if he were grateful to have a physical enemy to attack.

Frank blocked the flailing blows, lunging forward to grab Joe again. But a fist pounded through his guard, catching him full in the mouth. Frank flopped on his back, stunned, as his brother lurched to his feet and staggered toward the inferno.

Painfully pulling himself up, Frank wiped something wet from his lips—blood. He sprinted after Joe, blindly snatching at his T-shirt. The fabric tore loose in his hand.

Forcing himself farther into the glare and suffocating heat, Frank managed to get a grip on his brother's arm. Joe didn't even try to shake free. He just pulled both of them closer to the flames.

The air was so hot it scorched Frank's throat as he gasped for breath. He flipped Joe free, throwing him off balance. Then he wrapped one arm around Joe's neck and cocked the other back, flashing in a karate blow. Joe went limp in his brother's arms.

As Frank dragged them both out of danger, he heard the wail of sirens in the distance. We should never have come, he thought, never.

Just an hour before, Joe had jammed the brakes on the car, stopping in front of the mall. "So *this* is why we had to come here," he exclaimed. "They're having a rally! Give me a break, Iola."

"You knew we were working on the campaign." Iola grinned, looking like a little darkhaired pixie. "Would you have come if we'd told you?"

"No way! What do you think, we're going to stand around handing out Walker for President buttons?" Joe scowled at his girlfriend.

"Actually, they're leaflets," Callie Shaw said from the backseat. She leaned forward to peer at herself in the rearview mirror and ran her fingers hastily through her short brown hair.

"So that's what you've got stuck between us!" Frank rapped the cardboard box on the seat.

"I thought you liked Walker," said Callie.

"He's all right," Frank admitted. "He looked good on TV last night, saying we should fight back against terrorists. At least he's not a wimp."

"That antiterrorism thing has gotten a lot of coverage," Iola said. "Besides . . ."

". . . He's cute," Frank cut in, mimicking Iola. "The most gorgeous politician I've ever seen."

Laughter cleared the air as they pulled into a parking space. "Look, we're not really into passing out pamphlets—or leaflets, or whatever they are," Frank said. "But we will do something to help. We'll beef up your crowd."

"Yeah," Joe grumbled. "It sounds like a real hot afternoon."

The mall was a favorite hangout for Bayport kids—three floors with more than a hundred stores arranged around a huge central well. The Saturday sunshine streamed down from the glass roof to ground level—the Food Floor. But that day, instead of the usual tables for pizzas, burgers, and burritos, the space had been cleared out, except for a band, which was tuning up noisily.

The music blasted up to the roof, echoing in the huge open space. Heads began appearing, staring down, along the safety railings that lined the shopping levels. Still more shoppers gathered on the Food Floor. Callie, Iola, and four other kids circulated through the crowd, handing out leaflets.

The Food Floor was packed with people cheering and applauding. But Frank Hardy backed away, turned off by all the hype. Since he'd lost Joe after about five seconds in the jostling mob, he fought his way to the edges of the crowd, trying to spot him.

Joe was leaning against one of the many pillars supporting the mall. He had a big grin on his face and was talking with a gorgeous blond girl. Frank hurried over to them. But Joe, deep in conversation with his new friend, didn't notice his brother. More importantly, he didn't notice his girlfriend making her way through the crowd.

Frank arrived about two steps behind Iola, who had wrapped one arm around Joe's waist while glaring at the blond. "Oh, uh, hi," said Joe, his grin fading in embarrassment. "This is Val. She just came—"

"I'd love to stay and talk," Iola said, cutting Joe off, "but we have a problem. We're running out of leaflets. The only ones left are on the backseat of your car. Could you help me get them?"

"Right now? We just got here," Joe complained.

"Yeah, and I can see you're really busy," Iola said, looking at Val. "Are you coming?"

Joe hesitated for a moment, looking from Iola to the blond girl. "Okay." His hand fished around in his pocket and came out with his car keys. "I'll be with you in a minute, okay?" He started playing catch with the keys, tossing them in the air as he turned back to Val.

But Iola angrily snatched the keys in midair. Then she rushed off, nearly knocking Frank over.

"Hey, Joe, I've got to talk to you," Frank said, smiling at Val as he took his brother by the elbow. "Excuse us a second." He pulled Joe around the pillar.

"What's going on?" Joe complained. "I can't even start a friendly conversation without everybody jumping on me."

"You know, it's lucky you're so good at picking up girls," said Frank. "Because you sure are tough on the ones you already know."

Joe's face went red. "What are you talking about?"

"You know what I'm talking about. I saw your little trick with the keys there a minute ago. You made Iola look like a real jerk in front of some girl you've been hitting on. Make up your mind, Joe. Is Iola your girlfriend or not?"

Joe seemed to be studying the toes of his running shoes as Frank spoke. "You're right, I guess," he finally muttered. "But I was gonna go! Why did she have to make such a life-and-death deal out of it?"

Frank grinned. "It's your fatal charm, Joe. It stirs up women's passions."

"Very funny." Joe sighed. "So what should I do?"

"Let's go out to the car and give Iola a hand," Frank suggested. "She can't handle that big box all by herself."

He put his head around the pillar and smiled at Val. "Sorry. I have to borrow this guy for a while. We'll be back in a few minutes."

They headed for the nearest exit. The sleek, modern mall decor gave way to painted cinderblocks as they headed down the corridor to the underground parking garages. "We should've caught up to her by now," Joe said as they came to the first row of cars. "She must be really steamed."

He was glancing around for Iola, but the underground lot was a perfect place for hide-and-seek. Every ten feet or so, squat concrete pillars which supported the upper levels rose from the floor, blocking the view. But as the Hardys reached the end of the row of cars, they saw a dark-haired figure marching angrily ahead of them.

"Iola!" Joe called.

Instead of turning around, Iola put on speed.

"Hey, Iola, wait a minute!" Joe picked up his pace, but Iola darted around a pillar. A second later she'd disappeared.

"Calm down," Frank said. "She'll be outside at the car. You can talk to her then."

Joe led the way to the outdoor parking lot, nervously pacing ahead of Frank. "She's really angry," he said as they stepped outside. "I just hope she doesn't—"

The explosion drowned out whatever he was going to say. They ran to the spot where they'd parked their yellow sedan. But the car—and Iola—had erupted in a ball of white-hot flame!

Case #2
Evil, Inc.

When Frank and Joe take on Reynard and Company, they find that murder is business as usual.

THE FRENCH POLICE officer kept his eyes on the two teenagers from the moment they sat down at the outdoor café across the street from the Pompidou Center in Paris.

Those two kids spelled trouble. The cop knew their type. *Les punks* was what the French called them. Both of them had spiky hair; one had dyed his jet black, the other bright green. They wore identical black T-shirts emblazoned with the words *The Poison Pens* in brilliant yellow, doubtless some unpleasant rock group. Their battered, skintight black trousers seemed ready to split at the seams. And their scuffed black leather combat boots looked as if they had gone through a couple of wars. A gold earring gleamed on one earlobe of each boy.

What were they waiting for? the cop wondered. Somebody to mug? Somebody to sell drugs to? He was sure of one thing: the punks were up to no good as they sat waiting and watchful at their table, nursing tiny cups of black coffee. True, one of them looked very interested in any pretty girl who passed by. But when a couple of girls stopped in front of the table, willing to be friendly, the second punk said something sharp to the first, who shrugged a silent apology to the girls. The girls shrugged back and went on their way, leaving the two punks to scan the passing crowd.

The cop wished he could hear their conversation and find out what language they spoke. You couldn't tell kids' nationalities nowadays by their appearance. Teen styles crossed all boundaries, he had decided.

If the cop had been able to hear the two boys, he would have known instantly where they were from.

"Cool it. This is no time to play Casanova," one of them said.

"Aw, come on," the other answered. "So many girls—so little time."

Their voices were as American as apple pie, even if their appearances weren't.

In fact, their voices were the only things about them that even their closest friends back home would have recognized.

"Let's keep our minds on the job," Frank Hardy told his brother.

"Remember what they say about all work and no play," Joe Hardy answered.

"And *you* remember that if we make one wrong move here in Paris," Frank said, "it'll be our last."

Sitting in the summer late-afternoon sunlight at the Café des Nations, Frank was having a hard time keeping Joe's mind on business. He had no sooner made Joe break off a budding friendship with two pretty girls who had stopped in front of their table, when another one appeared. One look at her, and Frank knew that Joe would be hard to discourage.

She looked about eighteen years old. Her pale complexion was flawless and untouched by makeup except for dark shading around her green eyes. Her hair was flaming red, and if it was dyed, it was very well done. She wore a white T-shirt that showed off her slim figure, faded blue jeans that hugged her legs down to her bare ankles, and high-heeled sandals. Joe didn't have to utter a word to say what he thought of her. His eyes said it all: Gorgeous!

Even Frank wasn't exactly eager to get rid of her.

Especially when she leaned toward them, gave them a smile, and said, "Brother, can you spare a million?"

"Sit down," Joe said instantly.

But the girl remained standing. Her gaze flicked toward the policeman who stood watching them.

"Too hot out here in the sun," she said with the faintest of French accents. "I know someplace that's cooler. Come on."

Frank left some change on the table to pay for the coffees, then he and Joe hurried off with the girl.

"What's your name?" Joe asked.

"Denise," she replied. "And which brother are you, Joe or Frank?"

"I'm Joe," Joe said. "The handsome, charming one."

"Where are we going?" asked Frank.

"And that's Frank," Joe added. "The dull, businesslike one."

"Speaking of business," said Denise, "do you have the money?"

"Do you have the goods?" asked Frank.

"*Trust* the young lady," Joe said, putting his arm around her shoulder. "Anyone who looks as good as she does can't be bad."

"First, you answer," Denise said to Frank.

"I've got the money," said Frank.

"Then I've got the goods," said Denise.

The Hardys and Denise were walking through a maze of twisting streets behind the Pompidou Center. Denise glanced over her shoulder each time they turned, making sure they weren't being followed. Finally she seemed satisfied.

"In here," she said, indicating the entranceway to a grime-covered old building.

They entered a dark hallway, and Denise flicked a switch.

"We have to hurry up the stairs," she said. "The light stays on for just sixty seconds."

At the top of the creaking stairs was a steel door, which clearly had been installed to discourage thieves. Denise rapped loudly on it: four raps, a pause, and then two more.

The Hardys heard the sound of a bolt being unfastened and then a voice saying, *"Entrez."*

Denise swung the door open and motioned for Frank and Joe to go in first.

They did.

A man was waiting for them in the center of a shabbily furnished room.

Neither Frank nor Joe could have said what he looked like.

All they could see was what was in his hand.

It was a pistol—and it was pointed directly at them.

**And don't miss these other exciting all-new adventures
in THE HARDY BOYS CASEFILES**

Case #3
Cult of Crime

High in the untamed Adirondack Mountains lurks one of the most fiendish plots Frank and Joe Hardy have ever encountered On a mission to rescue their good friend Holly from the cult of the lunatic Rajah, the boys unwittingly become the main event in one of the madman's deadly rituals—human sacrifice.

Fleeing from gun-wielding "religious" zealots and riding a danger-infested train through the wilderness, Frank and Joe arrive home to find the worst has happened. The Rajah and his followers have invaded Bayport. As their hometown is about to go up in flames, the boys look to Holly for help. But Holly has plans of her own, and one deadly secret.

Available in May 1987.

Case #4

The Lazarus Plot

Camped out in the Maine woods, the Hardy boys get a real jolt when they glimpse Joe's old girlfriend, Iola Morton. Can it really be the same girl who was blown to bits before their eyes by a terrorist bomb? Frantically searching for her, Frank and Joe are trapped in the lair of the most diabolical team of scientists ever assembled.

Twisting technology to their own ends, the criminals create perfect replicas of the boys. Now the survival of a top-secret government intelligence organization is at stake. Frank and Joe must discover the bizarre truth about Iola and face their doubles alone—before the scientists unleash one final, deadly experiment.

Available in June 1987.